Daniel Watson
Berkley's Bastards Book 6

KATHI S. BARTON

This is a work of fiction. Names, characters, places, and incidents are products of the author's imagination or are used fictitiously and are not to be construed as real. Any resemblance to actual events, locations, organizations, or persons, living or dead, is entirely coincidental.

World Castle Publishing, LLC
Pensacola, Florida
Copyright © 2024 Kathi S. Barton
Paperback ISBN: 9798891262546
eBook ISBN: 9798891262553
First Edition World Castle Publishing, LLC, July 29, 2024
http://www.worldcastlepublishing.com

Prologue

Daniel looked over the paperwork again. Caleb Anderson was making too many waves for him to ignore. He was going to have to go and see what the man wanted, and soon, before he took too many more steps into finding him. He had a delicate balance right now and was afraid that someone other than him would get hurt. He didn't want it to be Caleb or the other men that he'd claimed as family.

"Danny, what do you know about a house explosion on Dewy Street?" He said that he hadn't heard anything. "House and two victims destroyed. The only thing that they do know for sure is that the neighbors, about three miles away, said they smelled gas. Would they be able to smell it from that far?"

"I suppose so." He put his paperwork back in his drawer and turned to the kid who was supposed to be his assistant. The only thing he'd been able to assist him with was a migraine from hell and annoying the fuck out of him. "Have you sent anyone out there yet? To see if it's true or not?"

"I should do that, huh?" Daniel didn't bother telling him that he should have sent someone the moment he heard the rumor. "I'll send out a crew."

"You do that, moron." As he was picking up his paperwork again, putting all his things into his briefcase, Daniel was sort of sad that this was going to be his last day. Doing undercover work for the Bureau was fun most of the time, but he'd learned a great deal about small-town news organizations by being here for the last four months.

Sending off his report, he was putting his things in his car when he saw the firetruck race by him. Must have been true, he thought as it was headed toward the little street that had been mentioned. Pulling out into the little bit of traffic, he was nearly into the street when a full-sized white van pulled in front of him. Putting his hand on his weapon, he waited to see what was going on.

"Doctor Watson, I presume." The man laughed, and Daniel rolled his eyes. He said that he'd been wanting to say that for months. "I have a male in here that is in need of your help."

"What sort of help?" He was getting into the van's back doors when someone got out on the other side and got into his car. A medical team of two was in the van with the man, and he could see that he'd been shot. "Do we have a place to work from?"

"Yeah, we're headed there now. Hang on." He did. Knowing this particular driver as being a full-on idiot, he watched as the man's blood pressure was being taken. Then, when they were stopping at what he assumed was a stop light, he had a chance to look at the wound and assess it. "Four minutes."

In less time than that, he was cutting the man open and removing the bullet. While he was being stitched up by the med team, he gave the man something for infection and pain after ascertaining that he'd not been provided either in the few minutes that he'd been in the van. Christ, this kid must be important if—

"Cassie? Cassie? Christ, she's bleeding too." They were in front of the house when she was scooped up and taken inside. The man would be taken care of as well, but he needed to see what he could do for the young woman. The bullet had entered her left shoulder and was still in there. Whoever had shot this couple, they had missed the spot twice. Hell was going to be paid. He'd bet anything.

It took him nearly an hour to get the woman to the point where he didn't think she was going to die. It had been touch and go there for a little bit. She had coded twice. Opening her chest up in a strange house without any precautions was the only thing he could do, as it turned out. The bullet had nicked her aortic artery, and she was bleeding internally. Lucky for her and him, the house had the equipment to keep her alive.

Sitting next to the two people, he didn't bother asking who they were. If they had wanted him to know, they would have told him by now. Instead, he looked over the paperwork that he'd brought with him when he'd gotten into the van.

"Did you find any misdealings there?" His boss, FBI Director Charles Dow, sat down next to him in another chair. "Not that I don't think it could happen, but the town is just too…I don't know, Disney-like for there to be foul play there."

"You'd think that, wouldn't you. But no, I didn't find that any of the allegations were true. The newspaper is above reproach, and they have a good community thing going on, too. It's just like you said, very Disney-like." Daniel got up and checked on the female. "I don't know that you're going to tell me anything, but these two were from there, right? Her clothing had a real-estate name on them, and he was dressed like you. What gives, if I can ask?"

"She is Cassie, Cassandra Blake. FBI. You might have heard about her when her husband was murdered right in front of her. Then the man is her

brother, Bradley Benson. He does work for us, too."
He asked if she was the one who had had the nervous
breakdown. "That's her. She's been working for us
under the guise of video surveillance for the realtor
by the name of Alder. I'm not sure how much either
of them knows about what happened today, but they
were leaving a job when someone opened fire on the
two of them. As you were able to figure out, she'd not
known that she'd been shot until she was in the van.
They're tight, the two of them."

"Okay, that explains who they are, but what are
they? I'm assuming since everything moved so quickly
that they're important in some way." He only nodded.
"Okay, closed-mouthed. I'm all right with that. It was
my last day at the newspaper office anyway. Can you
at least tell me where I'm headed next?"

"Yes. You're not going to like it." He looked
at the people in the beds and then back at his boss. "I
need someone to watch over them until they're healed
enough to take care of themselves. And I have the
perfect spot for you to do it. You get to meet up with
your long-lost family, too."

"Caleb Anderson." Charles nodded. "Why
him? I mean, there has to be a better place than a family
member's home? Don't you have any safe houses that I
could stay at with them? I mean, I'm not even sure that

the two of us are related."

"You are. You're his half-brother." He took the paperwork that was being held out to him. "You remember his mother, don't you? Abigail Anderson?"

"Yes." He did, too. Abby had been a good friend of his when— "She's his mother? Caleb is related to Abby Anderson? Christ, now I know why he's like this, not leaving shit alone when he couldn't find me. He's just like her."

"Thank you." The large man came into the room with him. There was no mistaking that they were related. When Caleb sat down, he looked at Charles. "He called me early last week when he found out that I've been looking for you. I had to pull a few strings to even get as much information that I had on you to come through. Then, about two hours ago, he called me again and told me that not only were you in town but that you needed me to help you. Welcome to the family, Daniel. We've all been waiting for you."

"Do you have any idea what we're doing here? Why I've been trying to avoid you? I'm an undercover FBI agent who is about as close to death as anyone gets on a daily basis and who works with bad people. I could very well get your entire family killed." Caleb told him that they were his family, too. "Look, this is a bad idea. I don't know these two people here, but they've been targeted to be killed, and the kind of people that do that sort of shit in broad daylight won't give a shit if you have six or six hundred people protecting you. They'll plow through you like you're nothing." Charles got up and left them there. It was then that he looked at his half-brother when he laughed.

"We have help." Daniel got up and started to pace. "My mother, she knew about you. I found some information about you that I didn't with the rest of them. Just notes on things. How you became so good at your job. She said that you have an ability that no one knows about."

Daniel stopped pacing and turned to look at the other man. Then he looked around to see if anyone had heard. While he knew that the room was being recorded, it wouldn't get shit while he was there. Not any mikes, cameras, or cell phones would work. It's why he didn't carry one. Nor wear a watch.

"What did she tell you? I've not seen her in a long time. How is she doing?" Caleb told him that she had passed away seven months ago from cancer. "Oh, I'm so sorry. She was a brilliant woman and one that I loved more than my own mother at times. I didn't know. I had no way of—You have my deepest condolences, Caleb. She was a wonderful woman."

"She was. And she made me promise that I'd

find all my brothers. You were the last one." Caleb laughed. "You'd not believe the shit that we've gone through with each of them. Sebastian was the last to join us before you had a mobster after him. Whatever we need to do, Daniel, to keep you safe, we're going to get through it. I promise."

He didn't bother telling him that it wasn't good to make promises like that when he didn't know what was going on. It was like the brother and sister that he was watching over now. Who knew what sort of shit was going to come about with having them around too.

"It's going to be hell. I hope you understand that." Caleb said that he'd been told it was going to be the worst yet. "That's about as accurate as it can get. I've been in and out of places that would make your hair turn white, as the saying goes."

They talked for the next hour. Not on any kind of plan to get them to his home. Not about what might be coming after the two on the beds with all sorts of shit hooked up to them. Caleb told him about his wife and brothers. The children and what they were up to. How his grandparents were helping out with projects around town that he might have heard of.

Daniel was impressed. All the good works that were going on around town were something that Caleb had a hand in. He'd not even realized that they were in the same town until today. All he'd had to do was walk down the street from the building he was working in and find his brother. Christ, talk about a small world. They had been together for the last few months, and neither of them knew a thing about the other.

When he was given a note, Daniel waited for him to read it before he let his tension go. Caleb looked at him, smiling when he handed him the note.

"Tabby is my wife. You'll learn not to mess with her. Or not. She'll love you anyway. But she's sort of firm about things. Well, you'll figure it out. She said that the basement has been converted into your lab of sorts and that you should come home with me and the other two." He asked him where he was going to be staying. "With us. Everyone in town knows that I've been looking for you. Most of the people won't even equate you with the man at the newspaper office. You didn't get out much, I'm to understand."

"No. I was working." Caleb stood up. "We're going now? To your home? I mean, this is a huge undertaking. How will you get the young couple there into your home?"

"It'll be a piece of cake." He wished he had the confidence that Caleb had. He'd never had an easy move in all his life and was sure that this wasn't going to be any different. Going out to the garage, he started

laughing when he saw the setup that was going on.
Yes, he thought, it was going to be a piece of cake with
this man in charge.

~*~

"Mister, I'm not coming down outta this tree until you
swear to me that that cur dog is out of sight. He already
done did bite me once. I don't like donating my blood
to nobody, especially not cur dogs." Daniel let himself
laugh at the little boy in the tree. "You just go on now,
Mr. Sebastian, and I'll be fine and dandy."

"Can I help?" Daniel had yet to meet any of the
others but Caleb as his family, so he put out his hand
to Sebastian, a man who could be his twin. "I think that
we're brothers."

"You don't know that you're brothers? Sheesh,
Mister. I got me five sisters, and they make for sure that
everyone knows that they're related to me. They're all
bigger and older than me, too." The little boy looked at
him. "Yeah, I can see that you're his brother, so don't
be thinking nobody else is gonna notice it."

"I didn't get to meet him when I came to town
yesterday. We all have the same father, but we've not
been together before." Luke, he found out the boy's
name and said that was nice for them all. "I guess.
Where is the cur dog?"

As if he'd summoned the pooch, he came

barking at them from around the corner. As soon as Sebastian told him to lay down, it did. Daniel was trying to hold back his laughter when Luke told the other man that he only minded big people, not little kids with teeth holes in his leg.

"He thinks you smell good to him." Luke told him that wasn't helping. "No. I suppose not. I'm not saying that you did anything, but could he have a reason for wanting to chomp on your legs? I mean, he doesn't look to me like a mean dog."

"I had to do it. My momma," Luke looked at Sebastian, then back at him before continuing again. "She's having herself a bad day. Dad, he knocked her around a bit and took all the money in the house again. I'm not asking for money, Mr. Sebastian. I'm just telling this man here, your brother, why the dog hates me. I was feeding him, you see. Putting out the scraps for him to munch on. You don't know what he looked like before I started doing that. All his ribs were fighting to be on the outside of his skin rather than where they're supposed to be. But momma, she got it in her head that we couldn't feed a cur dog—I don't even know what that means—no more on account of dad taking all the food money. Again."

"Is your momma all right?" Luke told him that she was in the hospital with his sisters. "All right. We'll come back to that. This dog, he's usually friendly to you, is he?"

"He is. Sometimes, when it's raining out, I bring him into my room and hide him away. My daddy, he'd have himself a conniption if he were to hear about that part. Woo Eee doggie. I'd be hurting." Daniel was having so much fun that he didn't want to leave, so he said he'd help the little boy and dog out. "The dog don't need much in the way of help, mister. He just needs to not be chomping on the hand that feeds him."

"Do you think perhaps you smell like your dad, and he's smelling him instead of you?" Daniel looked at Sebastian while Luke was thinking things over. "I was looking for Caleb and Tabby. I need to talk to them about something important. Do you know where they might be?"

"I know where Tabby is. She's with the other women out looking for a building to have the school's fair days in. They're just down the street at City Hall getting permits and standards that they're going to need." He asked about Caleb. "He should be with Joey. That's the last place I knew anything about either of them."

A thick jacket hit him on the head, and he looked up at Luke. "That's my daddy's. He said he wanted me to drop it off to be dry-cleaned. I put it on so that I'd not lose it. You think that's all it was, Mister?" He said the only way to find out was to test it on the dog. "I'm not going to be happy if you've been funning with me about this. He already bit me once today."

Once Luke was out of the tree, he could see how badly the boy had been knocked around, too. Telling him to put his hand out to the dog earned him a look, but he had confidence in the plan that he'd laid out for him.

The dog was growling at the back of his throat, but he did inch his way to Luke. Almost as if he would have given up, the dog jumped into the little boy's arms and was trying to lick his face off. The giggling little boy and the happy pup were just what he needed right now.

"Now that he's not going to chomp on you anymore, do you mind if I have a look at your wound? I don't want him to lose you again because you got an infection." Setting the two of them on the sidewalk, he cautiously looked at not just the superficial bite mark but also as many wounds on his arms and legs as he could. "I think we should all pay a visit to the hospital to make sure you're up to date on your shots. We can check on your mom and sisters while we're at it."

"You a doctor or something?" He said he was a doctor. "We sure could use a doctor in my family.

Dad comes around with his fists, all ready to do some hurting, and you could patch us up. Momma gets the most beating around. So does Serenity, but she hits him back now so he don't mess with her too much. Momma would too. She used to anyways. But since she's got the cancer, it's hard on her to defend herself." Luke looked up at the two of them. "I don't know what I'm going to do if I lose her. She's the best momma there ever was."

"She sounds like it." They took a hand each, and the three of them, with the dog following right behind, walked down the street. Sebastian said he had parked his car down here when he'd seen Luke up the tree. That was when he saw Caleb. "I have to talk to Caleb for just a minute. Do you think you guys could wait for me to go with you? I'd like to have a couple of tests run while—just give me a few minutes."

He was prepared for the bear hug that he'd gotten every time he came upon Caleb. It was breathtaking, literally, as well as it really did make him feel quite a bit better about things in general. However, he didn't have good news this time, and he almost hated to let him go.

"I heard about it." Nodding, he told him he was so sorry. "I am as well. While they didn't give us any kind of information on the two of them, it's still tragic that they both passed away. The young woman, Cassie, she had lost a lot of blood, you said, and the young man, Bradley, he was hurt pretty badly."

"If you don't mind me asking, how did you know?" He told him that his butler had gone to check on him and had heard him talking to someone about it. "I guess I could have been more discreet about it. I'm sorry that you had to find out that way. While I didn't really hold out much hope for the young woman, as you said, she'd lost a great deal of blood. I did hope for the young man to make it."

"Do you know what happens now?" He said that they'd make arrangements to have their bodies picked up for them. "No. I mean, I'm glad that is going to be taken care of. I meant about their killers. Do you know anything about if they've found them or not?"

"Several factions are taking credit for the deaths, though they don't say who they killed or where, so we're not putting much out there on that. I know that the president has his best men working on finding them. It happened on our soil, and he'll make sure that doesn't happen again. The two of them, brother and sister, from what I've been able to figure out, have lost a great deal in working for the government. I guess we'll just have to wait and see what else comes to us about it. I just don't know."

"Thank you for telling me." He got another hug. "You'll be staying, right? I mean, you just got here, and I'd hate to lose you so soon."

"I'm retired. I mean, I was retired before I came here. It was an easy assignment so that I could get my last fifteen days so that I could have my full retirement." Caleb smiled. "That's not to say that I might not get called in for something on this. Being on the scene when it first happened is about all the help I've been able to give them. But I was first on the scene, and I'm not sure what that will mean for the president."

"I'll have a talk to him." Daniel laughed, but Caleb didn't. He was never sure about this man. He'd never play against him in any game of life or just a board game. He held himself out there like he didn't have a care in the world, but once you got to talking to him, you saw a whole other part of him that he thought very few people did.

Going back to where he'd left Sebastian and Luke, he got into the car with them. As they were headed to the hospital, he thought about being a part of this growing family. He knew about Caleb and the others. Much more than he thought that they did about each other, and he was afraid that someone or something might happen to them. They were, he'd come to discover, just as friendly and nice as he'd read about them.

They pulled into the lot and went inside to the emergency department. There didn't seem to be a lot going on, but there were people waiting in the waiting room. A lot of them, about forty people. Daniel asked to see who was in charge.

"Nobody is." He didn't think that was right but asked again who was in charge of this shift in this department. "Are you deaf as well as stupid? Nobody. Fill out the paperwork over there on that kiosk thing and sit down. We'll get to you when we get to you."

He turned and looked at Sebastian, who looked as shocked as he felt. Going to the kiosk, he spoke quietly to Sebastian while trying to figure out how to handle this. He asked him if Caleb had any pull here.

"Yes. So does his grandparents. Want me—let me reword that. It would be my pleasure to call them and have them come here. The president of the hospital was terminated about a week ago. I don't have any idea what for, but I'm beginning to get a clearer picture now." Luke said he'd been turned away the other day when he'd come to see if his friend had broken his arm. "What happened to him?"

"He got himself an infection from the break, and they had to run him up to a bigger hospital. Sure is a shame, too. His family can't see him that far away."

Daniel hadn't heard anything about the hospital around here. Not even working about as close to it as he had. He wanted to think that it was a one-time thing, but it was slowly becoming apparent that this was the norm for here. "You gonna get them in trouble? I hope that they don't know that my mom is in here. They'll take it out on her if they do. Or maybe she'll get better care. They been holding her pain stuff, Sen told me."

Enough was enough. Calling Caleb while Sebastian called Caleb's grandparents, he laughed when he heard that someone was calling in the wives. Just the little bit of time that he'd spent with Tabby, he knew better than to fuck around with her. She was the sweetest little thing, but she had a fire in her that could burn down a house at fifty paces.

Caleb showed up first. No one even blinked an eye when he asked who was in charge. They told him the same thing that they'd said to him. Nobody. This time, however, she sounded out each syllable like it was something she wasn't fond of repeating.

When the grandparents showed up, it was iffy if they were going to be arrested. Mrs. Anderson was well up into the face of the woman behind the check-in counter, and she wasn't backing down, not even when security showed up. A sorrier bunch of men and women he'd ever seen, too.

After two more hours, he found himself sitting in the room of Olivia Branch. When Luke had said that his mother was dying, he hadn't mentioned that it might be as soon as today. It hadn't helped the woman to have been a punching bag for her husband, either. The daughters, five of them, were more protective of their mother and brother than he'd seen national security types protecting something.

"I don't have long, do I, Doctor?" He shook his head, and two of the girls stood up and dragged Luke along with them. "They're all I have in the world, and now I'm going to leave them to their father. Do you know of anyone who can take care of them for me? Just until my sister and Aunt can get here. I called them, but, well, money is tight everywhere. I was saving for them to send them money, but Burt took it all when he wanted to go and celebrate."

"What did he have to celebrate, Mrs. Branch, that was more important than your family having food on the table?" She said that he didn't pass that along to her, then laughed. "Luke takes after you in finding fun in about everything, I think."

"He's a good boy. Burt, he don't like him none because he's smart and corrects him all the time. Luke, he don't show off and talks like he's got not one brain cell in that noodle of his, but he's brilliant. Going to be ten next month and already done with high school. He's afraid his daddy will find out that he's really smart and make him find a job. My poor baby." The older daughter, Sen is what she went by, sat down on the other side of her mom and took her hand. "This one here, too, is brilliant. All of them are but Luke and Sen here, they've been the smartest of them all. Smart enough, too, that she won't marry anybody her daddy brings around because he said so."

"I don't live with them when he's home. I guess I thought that I could do more good than not if I had a job. I do, but it doesn't matter how much I bring to Mom and the others. Dad seems to know and takes it all." She told him that she was twenty-seven. "Though there are times when I feel like I'm twice that."

They talked to each other while Olivia dozed in and out. It really wasn't much longer for her to live. He'd been able to give her morphine to help with the pain, but she was almost too weak to do much more than moan. His heart broke for the little family, and he felt like he needed to do more.

What that would be wasn't anything that he could put his finger on. When Caleb showed up with food and the other kids, he helped Luke get his food loaded up on his plate and sit on the other bed. He ate with them as it had been a long time since breakfast, he told the little boy.

"Momma isn't going to come home this time, is she?" Daniel shook his head. "I didn't think so. She's worn out, isn't she? I don't want her to suffer anymore, but I don't want her to leave me either."

"She'll never leave you, Luke. Your mom will be with you for the rest of your life. She'll be watching over you. And every time you think of doing something you have to think hard on, you just ask yourself, what would my mom think if I did it this way. Or what would she do if she were in this place in my life? Every day, without her being right there beside you, you'll think about her, and she'll be right there guiding you." Luke hugged him, and he held him tightly while he thanked him for that. "You're so very welcome. I do the same with my mom every day, too. It's like she's my little angel right there on my shoulder, guiding me to do the right thing."

Luke held onto him for about twenty minutes before he realized that he'd fallen asleep. After he got him adjusted around so that he could lay him on the other bed, Alex helped him by covering up her brother.

"That's the nicest thing you could have done for him. He's been worried about that for weeks now, knowing that Mom was coming to an end. But you helped him. I can't thank you enough." He said that it had been his pleasure. "Doctor Watson, if you'd like to stay with us tonight here at the hospital, that would be great. Not as a doctor but as a friend. I think of you already as that."

"Yes, I'll stay."

Chapter 1

Daniel wasn't sure what he should be doing. He knew that if someone came into the emergency department that he could take care of them. For the last three weeks, he'd been organizing the hospital so that when they did find someone to run it, they could step into the role without having to search for every little thing. At least not in the office and this department, anyway.

Sure, he'd made his mark on it. Putting things together the way that he wanted it. But it was organized, unlike most of the other departments in the big hospital. Making his way to the front desk, he asked the woman sitting there, a woman who had been hired to only run the department, if there had been any calls out.

"No. Not as yet. Which, if you ask me, is good. The less we have to deal with until we get fully staffed, the better. Have you figured out why the head of this place fired so many staff before he left? I have a feeling it was him getting the last word in. The man was nothing if not vindictive." He had noticed a couple of days ago that she, like a lot of the staff that had been brought in, was armed. The Feds had come in and 'helped' with the staffing of not just the staff but had replenished the departments with doctors and nurses to help get the place back up and running. Even Sebastian's family, the Romans—a powerful Italian family had helped by having relatives come in and be staff, too.

The Romans had been the most powerful mobster family around for decades. They were still powerful and worldwide in their works. But when Parker, the patriarch of the family, had taken over decades ago and was father to three sons who were running the empire now, he had made them a giving family rather than one that only took and murdered. They were giving back; he thought a great deal more than was taken by them. After setting up shelters and clinics all over the country, they had settled in and began helping with anything and everything that they'd been asked to help with. Tabby and Caleb, his half-brother, had brought them in when they asked to be able to help. His family, he thought, was one of the more giving families than he'd ever seen. Daniel smiled when spotting Luke when he entered the emergency room door and spotted him.

"Hello, Mr. Daniel. I have a leash for Orange now. He's all right with waiting outside until I leave.

Thanks for making sure that he has food and water when we come to visit. He's getting kinda fat, but I think he's really happy." He got a hug from the young man. "You said that you wanted to check on my arm today. I didn't know you'd be in here."

"I'm the doctor on duty today. Who brought you here? Is Sen with you?" He said that she was parking the car. "Good. I don't like that you're still without a coat, but you said that you have one at the house. Aren't you cold?"

It had worked out really well with Luke and his five sisters living with him. The house that he'd gotten from Caleb—more like a flipping hotel to him, it had fourteen bedrooms as well as a butler's house. He'd been making use of it while the women and Luke made good use of his house. Besides, they were cooking for him, and he couldn't think of a single reason to have them looking for another place.

"Nah. I've been cold before. When my daddy was hanging around us he'd sell off my clothing that I'd get from the shelter place. By the way, Sen said to remind her about the receipts that she has for detergent and also donations." Daniel said he'd do that. "Good. Now don't forget. I won't get dessert tonight if you don't do this. She's depending on me to remember all kinds of stuff for my job. You know? It sure is nice to be able to walk around town without having to worry all the time, don't you think?" He agreed with him.

Burt Branch, their father, had been arrested not ten minutes after he'd been released the last time for drunk and disorderly conduct when his wife, Olivia, had passed away. He'd gotten out and went to the grocery store and tried to steal steaks and French fries. Not only was he run in again, but he had to wait for the judge to come in and hear his story before he could be released. Everyone was happier for those arrangements. Luke certainly was.

The sisters of Luke were working for the family, helping Tabby sort donated clothing so that it could be given away when people needed it. There were five of them, all mother hens when it came to their little brother. Luke would fuss about them, but he certainly loved them all. And Daniel couldn't blame him. They were about the nicest bunch of women he'd met in a long time. Between the five of them, he and his little buddy had been eating well every day since they moved in.

"I don't think that you're listening to me, Mr. Daniel. Are you getting all goo-goo over that woman at the desk? She's pretty but...well, she's pretty mean when she needs to be, too." He told him he was sorry, but he'd been thinking. "I've been doing that a lot, too. Anyway, my sister is taking me to the college tomorrow so that I can sign up for some college classes. I've not been hit once since my daddy was put in jail, you know. Even my sisters are healing up now, too. Do you know when my aunt and cousin are supposed to be coming to town?"

"I bet that they are. And no, not yet. I thought that they'd be here by now, but they had some trouble with the tickets that had been left for them at the airport." Daniel thought about what he'd heard about the mess up at the ticket counter but decided it wasn't his place to make a judgment about the two people. "Tabby said that you and your sisters have gotten all the donated things separated out and washed and dried. That has to be a great thing for the people that go there." Luke said that his sister was allowed to wash their clothing there as well. "That must be nice. You tell them that the washer and dryer that I purchased will be there tomorrow. Then they don't have to lug their things over there too. I certainly don't have enough dirty things to use it all that often." He'd gotten him a smaller set for the house he was using. It was working out well for the little bit that he was wearing. And it was close, too.

"I'll tell them that. I think that they feel bad about using the one in the donation place. It's a nice one, but like you said, they have to lug all their clothing in and out of the place, and it has about fifty stairs to it." They both laughed, knowing that the place only had about five steps, but they were steep. "Sen has a job interview with Mr. Caleb tomorrow, too. Did you know that?"

"Doesn't he know what she can do already? I mean, she's been working for him for two weeks now at the donation place." Luke told him what apparently his sister had told him. "Oh. Yes, I can see where he'd want to make it fair to everyone that was applying. Also, I do the same things here. Interview for a lot of different jobs that need to be filled up then put them where I think they'll work out. Good idea on his part but I guess he didn't get rich by being stupid. Caleb is smart for doing it that way if he has that many jobs that need to be filled in different areas around town. The hospital alone needs about three dozen more people working here."

Caleb, the man who had set out to find him and the other men who had been sired by Howard Berkley, had gathered them all up and made their lives a good deal better than they had ever been. Caleb's mom, Abby Anderson had made it so that her son had plenty enough resources to do what he needed to not just find them but to bring them here to live around him. Daniel had been the last of them. His mom, like the others, had been raped by Howard and left to raise him on her own.

His mom, like most of the other half-brothers, had passed on. He didn't think that his mom had ever been all that healthy even before she had him, and raising him on her own hadn't been all that easy on her. But, and he would be forever thankful to her, she had made him the man that he is today. Someone that people could depend on.

After getting Luke set up to have an x-ray of his arm, he looked them over and declared him well enough to start exercising it. The kid had been complaining about only being one-armed in trying to hold down a job. Daniel thought that at ten years old, he could hold off on working full time. The kid, he loved him to pieces and he had a charm about him that made him feel like he was on top of the world just by being around him.

When his cell phone rang, another gift from Caleb so that they could talk whenever they needed to, he answered with his name. Realizing that it was Tabby, Caleb's wife, he smiled, thinking about how happy he was that his brother had found himself such a wonderful person to live the rest of his life with.

"I just heard from Olivia's sister." He had to think a moment and remember that she was talking about Luke's mom. "Her name is Beatrice Miller, and her daughter is July. I have to admit something only to you, I don't know that I'm going to care for her. The aunt. She's kind of...how should I say this... She's a fucking bitch." He laughed and was happy that Luke had gone out to go help Ava, one of his sisters, clean the kitchen up at home. "I want everyone to be on their toes around her. She's been making comments about the kids that make me think that we shouldn't have bothered with contacting her. Ms. Miller is a great deal like her brother-in-law, Burt. A mean person."

"Did you ever hear what happened with the tickets that were waiting for them at the airport?" She explained to him how the mess-up had occurred. "How is that your fault? If she didn't get to the airport on time, I don't see how she can say that you were the one to mess their flight out. Yeah, I'm right there with you. I don't know that I'm going to like them either. She'd better not be a bitch to those kids. I know the older ones can hold their own, but not the two younger ones."

"Maybe she's just grieving. I know that it can make a person say and act differently than they normally did." He didn't believe that, and he was sure that Tabby didn't either. "Anyway, she's going to be here this evening. If you don't mind, we're going to meet up at your house when she arrives. We're sending a car for her since, according to her, she's going to need time to chill before meeting her sister's family. I'm all right with that. I don't want to be in a car with her for over an hour, either. I've made a couple of calls. Her plane will arrive at about four this afternoon. After they get their luggage then get here, it'll be around five-thirty or six. The caterers will be at your home about that time. They'll set up and clean up, too. I just don't want to have to deal with food since the weather has turned again. Did you know that it was supposed to be ninety today? Yesterday, it was forty. I don't care for the weather around here."

After making sure that he knew what he had to do when the caterers arrived and where the aunt was staying with her daughter, he told Sen when she came out of the elevator after her interview with Caleb. He also reminded her about the receipts, too.

He really liked this sister. Daniel loved them all, actually, but Sen and her sister Ava were the ones that he had spent the most time with at the house, being about his age. They were all smart, too, and could hold their own in a conversation.

"I don't remember her at all. I did remember my mom talking about her a couple of times. How they really didn't get along all that well. But since she's all mom had, she wanted her to come and see to Luke and Beth. They're the only two that aren't adults yet." Daniel asked her why she didn't adopt her brother. "I'd love to, I would. But mom didn't want me to be settled, she called it with my little brother if a man came along and wanted to marry me." She snorted.

"You don't think that anyone would want to marry you?" She did that twirl-around thing, showing him, he supposed what a man would be getting if he did. "I don't know if you're serious or not but I would think that any man would be thrilled to have a partner like you in life. You're smart, beautiful, and funny. And you have a readymade family right here."

They both laughed. That was another reason for him to like her a great deal. She never took anything seriously if she didn't have to. She and Luke were off-the-charts smart, both of them having graduated from high school before they were ten and started college right away. The other four sisters were smart, too, but they'd not graduated until they were twelve. It made him smile when he told anyone how brilliant his housemates were.

At three o'clock, he made his way home. While he was on call for the entire day, there hadn't been a single emergency in since he'd gotten there. The entire area had been told that if they had an emergency and could make it to one of the other hospitals in the area, to go there. The hospital was very short-staffed, and it would be a while before it was up to standards again, even with the extra help that was coming in from other hospitals.

Lucky for him, he didn't live all that far from the hospital and could walk home. The girls had been using his car since he'd gotten it. Or since his big brother had gotten him one. Caleb was an extremely generous brother.

~*~

Watching the trees as they swayed back and forth, she thought that she'd never realized how relaxing it could be to sit quietly and not fill her mind up with things that could have and should have been done. Looking to her right when the door opened, she stood up and carefully made her way to the room where she'd be doing her exercises in.

"You're doing very well, Major. I don't have to ask if you are keeping up with things. You're muscles are loosening up very nicely now." Cassie asked her if she'd heard from her boss. "No. Only in that, you're supposed to be given the best of care no matter what you have to say. I think that he's going to want you better sooner than you do."

"I didn't want to be better at all. That's the

problem." Cassie had been shot when her brother had been killed. Every day since she woke up from the operations that had saved her life, she wished that they would have just let her die along with him. Bradley had been her hero, her best friend and her brother like none other. "Did they tell you when I can get out of here? I'd like to go to his grave before the snow comes in. And is there any word on who it was that killed him?"

"No word on when you can leave here to go see his grave. I've been thinking that someone could take a picture of it for you. Cassie, you do understand that you've been declared dead as well, don't you? If you go snooping around, as I think you want to do, you could be caught and killed. No one wants that, I promise you." She nodded, then turned away from the woman. "I'm sorry, Cassie. I truly am. I know it won't be the same, but I'll go there after I leave here and take some pictures for you. And I'll ask in my report when you're going to be taken out of here."

"Please do." Being declared dead had more than likely saved her life along with the people that she'd been staying with. But she didn't want to live. There was nothing for her to live for. Not anymore. "I've lost so much, Connie. Everything when you think about the fact about how I'm living. Hiding away in the dark like an animal. I miss my brother."

Cassie lifted her legs as she was asked to do when the two of them settled into their routine. Exercising her body, trying to get back into the shape she'd been before was difficult for her. Not that she'd been all that out of shape before being shot at, but she just didn't have the will to do anything lifesaving. She'd lost so much that she didn't want to be sticking around to lose anymore.

First, her parents when she and her brother had been just teenagers. They'd been killed when the plane that they'd been riding in had simply dropped from the sky. It had been their anniversary that week and they'd planned to go back to the places that they'd seen on their honeymoon. They were on their way home when the plane crashed, killing all two hundred eighty-seven on board, including the crew.

After that, it was her husband. She'd met Albert on a job, and he had been killed as well. He'd been out of the country working on a project that she'd still never found out what it had been. His body was shipped home to her on the day of their wedding anniversary. Five years to the day, she'd had to put him to rest. She had a nervous breakdown that night, having to be hospitalized for six months until she was ready to face the world again. Now she's lost Bradley.

Bradley had been the only person in the world that had made her feel like living again. With his sense of humor and his ability to find something positive in every circumstance, she missed him more than anyone that she'd ever missed. She wished daily that she could lie down beside him and end her life to join all her family in the afterlife. If there was one. But people with more pull than she had had made it so that she had lived while everyone around her was gone. It broke her in ways that she didn't think she could stand.

The phone was ringing when she went into the little room she'd been using the most. There were no computers nor televisions in the place, not much in the way of furniture either. Just a couch in the living room that had a full-sized refrigerator stocked full of water and sodas. A bed with a matching dresser in her bedroom. There was no kitchen, not that she would have used it anyway nor was there anything that would help her connect with the outside world. And she liked it like that. Right up until she didn't. And the last two days had proven to her that she's not all that good with her own company.

Picking up the phone, she waited for the person on the other end to speak. When they said the code for the day, Harvey the Rabbit, she said her name. The man on the other end of the line was laughing, and she knew who it was immediately.

"You can't tell me that you're tired of the walls already, Major Blake. I had a hand in decorating them just for you." She told the president that it was the ugliest rooms that she'd ever been in. "Yes, well, we needed to act quickly. But I am sorry, honey. Connie said that you wanted to go to the grave site. I can't allow you to do that just yet, either. We're using every man that we have now in trying to find the person or persons that shot at you and Bradley. As soon as we have him, I'll personally take you there."

"I miss him." She sobbed a little, having a rough morning already, and now this. "I miss him so much, you can't imagine. I have no one left. No one to hold me when I'm down. Nothing."

"Oh, Cassie, honey, I'm so sorry. My heart hurts for you and all that you've lost. Let me do some things on this end, and I'll get back to you. I'm not saying that it will be able to go through, but I'll see what I can do for you." She cried more, thanking him for putting up with her. "You are the one that I should be thanking. Without your help, even as hurt as you were, we wouldn't be as far as we are now in finding the persons responsible. We'll get them. Sooner rather than later. I'm not going to allow two of my best agents to be shot at and one of them killed without using all the power that I have to find them. Let me call you back."

Cassie laid down on her bed and cried herself to sleep. She'd been doing that so much since she woke up here that she was sure that she had shed enough tears that she could fill a bathtub. She hurt. Not just from the injuries from being shot, but her entire body ached all the time because of how lonely she was.

Waking up to her phone ringing again, she didn't say anything again until Wilhelm Davis, the president, did. He told her that he had a plan, but she'd have to do exactly what she was told, or the mission would be aborted. He asked her if she could do that.

"Yes. Will I get to go to the grave?" He said so long as she listened to the people she'd be staying with. "I just don't know what to say. Of course, I'll listen. And I promise that I'll do what I'm told. Just to be able to get out and about for a minute would be more than I could have hoped for today."

By the time her dinner was brought to her, she was ready to go. Wilhelm told her that once things were set into motion—he'd been the one that briefed her on what was to happen—and it would need to happen quickly. As soon as the agents showed up at the place she'd been staying, they handed her a bag. Inside of it were clothing and a wig, plus a pair of glasses. Not for the sun, she'd been told, but for her to look like someone else. She was nearly giddy with excitement.

After getting dressed, she was ready to go to the airport. She hadn't realized how far she'd come when they moved her out of Caleb Anderson's home until just then. Taking a commercial flight had her seated next to one of the agents who was dressed similarly to how she was. Jeans and a nice shirt that he was wearing with a plaid shirt over it. Even his boots looked like he'd been shit-kicking, something that Bradley said a lot and didn't look shiny and new. For that matter, her clothing and boots didn't either.

The agent, Jim, handed her a small box and she was asked to wear the ring inside. She put it on and was surprised that it was a college ring. She'd been told that it had a tracker in it and that she was never to take it off.

Cassie had one of her own at home, but this one was for Brown, and she'd gone to Harvard. Slipping it on, she put her wedding rings that she still wore in the box as well and handed it back to him. It was the first time she'd removed her wedding rings since her husband had put them on her fingers all those years ago.

The trip wasn't all that long. Even before they landed, she could see the airport and some of the smaller planes that were there. She knew where she was, but keeping her excitement from alerting people around her that she was not a normal passenger, she continued to watch the goings on around her.

"See the family ahead of you? The women and the man?" She nodded at the whispered question in her ear. Another thing that she'd been given on the plane was an earphone. "The man is Daniel Watson. He actually was the one that saved your life. Those are his housemates. Cling to them like they're family. You're going to be the long-lost sister to them all. The youngest is Luke. He'll be accepting if the others are."

She had all their names ready when she came up to them, glad that she'd been given pictures and briefed on them as well. Doctor Watson simply shook her hand when introduced to him, but the women, five of them, were excited to see her. She had never been so wrapped up in hugs as she was from them. Even Luke acted like he'd not seen her in a while by hugging her tightly to his small frame. It was Serenity, Sen for short, who filled her in on things.

"Dad is in jail still. He won't be getting out until the judge comes to see him. Maybe another week, they said." She'd been prepared on that as well. Burt Branch had been beating on his children since they'd been born. And perhaps was indirectly responsible for the expedited death of his wife, Olivia. "We're going to be getting something to eat. I'm so glad that you're home finally."

They treated her like their long-lost sister. Not once did anyone give them a sideways glance unless they were marveling at the beauty of the women. Cassie knew that she was all right looking, but these women were amazing, beautiful women who were helping her get to see her brother's grave.

She was surprised that Doctor...she supposed she should call him Daniel like the others did, paid for lunch. She'd not been sure if she would have to pay for her own, but he treated her like he did the others. They all seemed to have a good relationship, and she hoped that she was fitting in. This was important to all of them. If she was caught, they'd all pay the price. It was why she was glad to see several of the secret service men and women lingering around the airport and restaurant, too.

They made two stops on the way home. The first one was to the grocery store, and she went in with them like part of the family. She couldn't believe how frugal they were about food. Even Luke, when told he could pick out any cereal that he wanted weighed his options like he was thinking how he'd win the lottery. He ended up getting a box of plain cornflakes that he knew everyone would share with him. She fell in love with him right then and there.

Cassie didn't have any money, she realized, when she got up to the counter with a basket of personal items. Daniel slipped her some cash, fifty dollars, just as she was thinking that she should have just stayed where she'd been and not embarrassing this little family. But he didn't make a big deal out of it, just handing her the money and walking away. She was able to purchase some flowers, just as the others had, with enough money left over to treat herself to a candy bar and share it with Luke.

The cemetery was next on their list of places to visit. She'd not realized that the children had lost their mother recently, and that was where they were headed. When Daniel held back, asking her to follow him but to keep moving, he took her right by her brother's gravesite.

She wanted to lay herself down on the grave and cry, she was so happy to see the marker with his name on it. Daniel stopped her, leaning over to take her foot up to his waist, and pretended to look at her ankle. Her hand was resting on the stone. Cassie knew that this was going to be as close as she was going to be able to get to his grave until the people were caught that had killed her hero.

"Thank you." He told her that it was his

pleasure and that her ankle looked like it was going to be all right. Nodding, not sure that she could speak to him right then, she reached for his hand, and he took it. "I'm a little emotional right now. I guess I missed him...them more than I thought that I would."

"Understandable. When we get back to the house, I have some photographs for you to look over. Nothing big, just some people that I was asked to ask you about. Also, there will be a cell phone for you to use as well." She nodded, and then he explained to the kids there, that Sen and Ava were about her age, so she had to stop calling them kids, that their aunt was coming in today. They all groaned. "Come on, guys. She came all this way. We can make her welcome, can't we?"

"Yeah, we're having all kinds of food too. Ms. Tabby is having all kinds of catering things brought to the house. We don't even have to clean up." She laughed. It felt good. Something that she'd not done in a very long time. "You need to laugh more, sis. It sure is a pretty sound coming from you."

"Thank you." They all touched the headstone of their mom as they left the flowers for her. The other flowers that had been there were taken away, and the ones that were still good were put on the graves of some of the others around the cemetery. Cassie put her hand on the headstone as well but said nothing out loud. Her heart was breaking again, but for the family that the woman had left behind.

As they were leaving the cemetery, going the same way that they'd come in, she watched as Luke, putting flowers on some of the graves that they passed put one on her brothers. She barely made it to the car before she broke down. Once in the limo, she leaned on Daniel and sobbed her heart out. The others hugged her, too, and it was the first time in longer than she could remember that Cassie felt like she could go on in the world.

They were all seated in the living room when the front doorbell rang. There was staff in the home, but it was Daniel who got up to answer the door. As soon as she heard the woman's voice, bitching about the right to the house, she got up and left the room as quickly and as quietly as she could. Once outside, she made her way to the butler's home, the one that Daniel was living in, and entered with the key that he'd given her. As soon as she was settled in with the television on, someone knocked on the door. It was a man in a nice suit coat, and he had some of the food that they were fixing in the big house next door. Thanking him, she put it all in the kitchen and sampled the cake first. It was just as delicious as it looked.

Chapter 2

Beatrice didn't care for the things that had been set up for them when they arrived. First and foremost, the family hadn't sent a private jet for them when she knew that they had one. Then there was the fact that their tickets weren't first class. Who would do that to people they invited to their home. Even bullying the man and woman that had been in the seats hadn't gotten her anywhere near the first seats. He'd paid for them, he told her. Like that made a big difference to her.

July, of course, was being a total sap and not wanting her to make a scene. Of course, she had to explain to her, once again, that saps finished last, and if you didn't make your mark in the world, then no one was going to take you seriously. It was a lesson that she'd been taught by her late husband, bless his soul.

The house was much nicer than she thought that it should have been. They were bragging she worked out in her head and that bothered her to no end. Trying to outshine her would get them nowhere quickly. Stupid people. Even though they were all dressed in jeans — she hated that kind of lowlife style, they looked expensive. Like they'd just come from some kind of beauty salon to make them look so special. But they were going to see that she wasn't easy to impress or fool. So when she was offered a seat, she turned her nose up at the man.

"Where is the boy? The one that everyone is expecting me to raise as my own." No one said anything to her but a kid did stand up. The child looked just like his mother. "You're scrawny, aren't you? And you don't look the least bit like my sister. Probably because she had some kind of sexual fling, and you're the result. I wouldn't put it past her. Olivia was never worth the spit that made her. Now she has a bunch of curs that she's expecting me to raise."

The girls stood up, but they didn't say a word. It was the man that spoke and his words sparked a fire in her that she actually was excited about. But no one told her to mind her words, and got away with it. Drawing back her hand to hit him, he pulled a gun from his back and put it down at his side, like he was testing her or something. Again, the excitement was there. Beatrice wasn't the least bit afraid of him shooting her. It was him thinking that he could, to her of all people, that pissed her off.

"Didn't anyone ever tell you that you don't

draw a gun or your pecker unless you plan on using it?" He pulled the gun up enough to put his second hand on it. However, before she could comment on him being a pussy, he racked the slide and then put it at her forehead this time. "What do you plan on doing? Killing me? Not fucking likely."

"We need to calm down." She'd not heard anyone else come into the room and turned to look at the newcomer who was interrupting her playtime. "My name is Caleb Anderson. This is my wife, Tabby. What do you mean by coming here and making accusations like that to Olivia's children? Not to mention your own sister. None, that's what. You'll sit down and shut up, or I'll have you on the next plane out of here. You're here because of my generosity and I have no trouble whatsoever in doing what is necessary to make sure you never see the kids again."

"Were you under the assumption that I wanted to see them anyway? I was summoned here because my sister died. If that wasn't bad enough, you didn't send me first-class tickets like you should have. Nor a plane like I asked for to get me here in time to be at her funeral. Christ, what a shitshow this has been. Now you expect me to, no doubt, take these kids with me so that they have a mother figure too — do I look stupid to you? I'm not." One of the girls asked why she'd made the trip here if she didn't want to take them home with her. "I'll take him in. I'm sure that there is some money around that can be used to keep him in clothing and shit. And I could use a good worker to clean up after myself and my own child. My sister might have been an idiot, but she knew how to take care of her children. How much is the policy for that I'm getting? I'm sure that it's for a goodly amount." The girls laughed. Beatrice wanted to slap the lot of them, but the gun was still out — not pointed at her any longer, but close enough that he'd use it on her if she tried to hurt them.

"She left it to Luke to be able to use when she passed away. No one can touch it but him when he's twenty-one." The girl laughed. "I guess it sucks to be you, don't you think? We'll have jobs, of course, and keep him in clothing like we are now. I couldn't care less if you took him or not. I'll raise him on my own if you don't. I believe we'd all like that better anyway."

Beatrice wanted to slap that smug look off her face so badly that her jaws hurt she was grinding her teeth so hard. When the man finally stepped back but did not put his gun away, she nearly moved to do it. However, the girl moved out of the room. That was when she smelled the food that was cooking. She'd refused to eat the food on the plane, not that any had been offered and now she was expected to eat with all of them.

Dinner wasn't the quiet affair that she wanted. They all spoke over each other, laughing and having a good time while she was seething about it all. They had obviously never heard the saying that children should never be heard when seen. Or something like that.

When a bowl of what she thought was mashed potatoes was passed to her, she told the man, she'd never caught his name, so she called him Gunner, asked her if she wanted some.

"Well?" He shoved the bowl at her then, and she had no choice but to take it. "You bastard. I'm used to being served my meals, not someone shoving food at me and expecting me to shovel food onto my own plate. Just give me some and move on."

"Fine." Instead of serving her, he passed the bowl around her to the person on her other side. Which happened to be Caleb something. She was so pissed that she could feel her blood pressure rising up, and when the kid laughed, she aimed all her anger at him.

"You'd better be enjoying yourself now, young man. When I get you home, you're going to learn your place and it will not be eating with the good people that I know, including myself. Why, as much as I've seen of you already, you'll be better off eating in the yard with the dogs. You're an ill-mannered little shit, and if I have to beat you, you're going to learn how to behave yourself." Jerking the next food that was being passed around, she ended up having green beans spilled on her new dress. Before she could think about what she was doing, she slapped Gunner in the face, flipping him backwards in his chair.

She was satisfied for all of a minute when Tabby came up from her chair and punched her in the face. Even as she was flying backward, Beatrice knew that she might well have bitten off more than she could chew with that woman. She was meaner and quicker than she was.

Waking up, Beatrice knew that she was in a hospital. Yelling for someone to come to her, her head felt like it was going to explode right off her shoulders. When July entered the little room she was in, she asked her what had happened.

"You mean the part where you ended up in here, Momma? Well, you hit Doctor Watson, and when he fell backwards, Ms. Anderson hit you. She hit you hard enough that you hit your head twice on the floor. You have a concussion as well as fifteen stitches in the back of your head from the floor." She said that she was suing. "They all thought you might say that, Momma, but since you hit first, the police are saying it was justified for you to be hit back. Also, Doctor

Watson is pressing—"

"Wait a minute. Who the hell is Doctor Watson? And what the hell does he have to do with anything?" July explained to her that he was the man whose house they'd been in and the man that she'd hit. "You mean Gunner? He owns that house? I won't believe that. Not even if there was proof. I'm supposing that he could afford something like that, being a doctor, but what I want to find out is what he's doing with my nieces there? Huh? Do you know that?"

July shrugged, something that she knew that she hated, but her head was splitting right now, and she couldn't think beyond getting out of there. Asking her daughter to go and get her some medications for her head, she showed her the button she needed to push. Pissed off more than she'd been in a long time, she felt her head pound all the harder and her belly churn up like it did when she drank some milk.

The alarm on something was going off over her shoulder, but she suddenly couldn't turn to scream at someone to turn it off. It was all she could do not to puke all over herself. But that happened, too, as she couldn't stop herself from being sick.

Two nurses rushed into the room and started telling her that she needed to calm down before she had a heart attack. They were standing too close to her, leaning over her and talking to her like she was an errant child. Her head popped, and just like that, Beatrice felt it pop behind her eyes and couldn't see for several seconds. The first nurse told her she had to remain calm.

"I've had plenty of heart attacks, and it's not done one thing to me. Back off. I know what it is that I have to do." She wasn't in the mood to do her breathing right then and was shocked to feel a pinch at her arm and the sudden rush of lightheadedness wash over her. "What have you done to me? Damn it."

Waking up the next time, she knew that something had happened. Not only was she in a room now but there were all kinds of machines all around her. Reaching up to jerk the nose cannula out of her nose, she felt the straps that were holding her down. Damn it all to fuck and back, what the hell were they—

"You've had a heart attack." Turning her head was difficult, but she finally made it work for her. She'd never been this exhausted before just moving around, but she looked at the girl sitting in the chair next to the bed. "I'm Serenity, Mother's oldest and not Burts child. I'm not going to bother with telling you what everyone calls me. You'll just call me what you want anyway. I remember you now. You've not changed a bit since I was a little girl. Have you? But you've had a heart attack. It did some damage, but not a great deal. But you'll have to be careful from now on that you don't get stressed. Also, take your medications. I'm assuming you think that you're above such things."

She couldn't speak, she discovered, and that had her trying to reach her mouth again. Jerking on the straps that weren't just on her arms but her legs too, Serenity smiled at her and told her that she was cuffed to the bed because she kept pulling out the things that were keeping her alive. Beatrice knew that she was above such things as medication.

"As I've said, you had a heart attack. Your left side is weaker than your right because you're partially paralyzed. By that, I mean that you will have to be in a wheelchair as well as someone to care for you while you undergo exercises that will at least bring yourself up to functioning." She laughed. "However, I can guess that you're not going to do anything of the sort and will still be a bitch when you are in a nursing home. That's entirely up to you, I suppose. Your daughter has gone home to rest. Not that you care about her all that much either, do you?"

"No." Her mouth felt heavy like she wasn't able to speak properly. When Serenity wiped her mouth, she was embarrassed to see that she'd been drooling. Christ, she was going to be impaired from this to the point that she was going to have to do just what the younger woman had told her. Telling her *no* again, the girl just laughed.

"No? Well, I guess that was expected as well. You won't get better unless you make yourself do what you're told. I actually hope that you don't. I've never liked you since I was a little girl, and you slapped me when I asked my mom for a glass of milk. Yes, I remember you very well. Plus, knowing that you're going to be in a nursing home thrills me to no end. Also, and this is the best news ever, you aren't going to be taking my little brother anywhere. We'll raise him ourselves." She couldn't make herself tell the bitch that she wasn't going to be doing any such thing because her mouth and face wouldn't work the way that she wanted it to.

All the while she was trying her best to get words out, she had missed the girl leaving. Damn it all the fuck. What was wrong with people nowadays? Stupid, that was it. They were all stupid.

She didn't know if the girl was telling the truth or not but thought maybe she was in deeper shit than she'd been before. Her body betrayed her like everyone else had. Beatrice realized that she should have been taking her medication instead of doing what she wanted. Of course there was no way that she was going to admit to that. Wondering where her daughter was—thinking that if she had to suffer, so did she—exhaustion slid over her, and it was too difficult to make herself stay awake.

When she woke again, feeling overwhelmed by memories of her childhood of all things. But with a hard jerk on her arm, she realized that she was still chained like a dog. Looking around while pressing buttons on the call button to get the nurse to come in here and release her, Beatrice turned the television on and off several times and had the volume so loud that it hurt her already pounding head. Finally, someone came into the room to help her.

"Mrs. Miller, what can I do for you? I know that you're not speaking well, so if you'd just let me ask you questions, with you blinking once for yes and two for no, we'll see if we can do anything for you." She blinked twice, not wanting to look like an old fool. "All right, you don't want to do it that way. I'm going to assume then. You need pain medication, I'm betting. I'll be right back with something for you."

Beatrice blinked so many times to tell her that she didn't want anything like that she felt as if her eyeballs were going to pop right out of her head. By the time the nurse returned, Beatrice was half sick with pain again. Glad for the medications now, she was drifting off when she remembered what it was that she'd wanted. She wanted someone to get the police. It was high time someone taught those bastards who did this to her a lesson.

~*~

"I took July to the airport. She's not going to return to take care of her mother. She did leave her banking and attorney information with me but she won't be back. And since the judge gave her power of attorney over her mother because of the heart attack, she said that she was going to live the life that she wished she'd had. I don't know what that means for the girl, but I wish her luck." Daniel laughed a little before he continued. "She also signed the paperwork for her mother that gives up any custody of Luke and his sister so that they can be adopted by their sisters. I think they'll do a great job in keeping him safe."

"I agree." They were sitting in the living room, just having a nice rest after the week that they'd had. Cassie had been to the cemetery twice more since arriving but had only been by the grave of her brother once. She found that she could live with that because it was close to where she was now.

Cassie didn't want to draw attention to the fact that she was there to see him. But with the pictures that someone had taken from her apartment, she had been able to grieve a little more since she'd been here. Having all the people around her was better than she'd ever expected. Family was a good thing, she thought.

"I'd like to speak to you about some things if you'd not mind. I know you've been through a great deal…what I mean is, I would…Would you have dinner with me?" The question startled her some, and she didn't answer him. Or couldn't, she didn't know which before he spoke again. "I've been thinking about you for a few days now and wondered if you'd like to have dinner with me. Just the two of us."

"Won't people see me? I mean, I'm always worried that someone will see me and everyone will be killed." He said that if she wore her glasses, she looked enough like Sen that she could pass as her sister, too. "I've noticed that. I wonder if that was why they picked your house for me to hide out."

"I volunteered. I found out that you had survived, for which I'm so grateful for that I said you could hide out here. With all the women here and you, you've blended in very well." She asked him about Sen. "What about her?"

"I thought that the two of you were seeing each other." He smiled at her and told her that they weren't. "Does Sen know this? I like her and don't want to step on anyone's toes right now. I have enough going on at the moment."

"I'm sure. When we first started out living here together, I was kind of hoping for some companionship with her. But it was too much like…she seems like my sister. Or something like that. The rest of them do as well. Like we're related in some close way." Daniel laughed again, telling her how he felt about the other woman. "We get along great. I think it has to do with the fact that we've been living in close quarters for so long that we've developed into sisters and brothers more than anything romantic."

"I'm not sure about…I've been married before. My husband was killed out of the country. I don't have any family left." He smiled and said that he only had family because Caleb had given him one. "Yes, I heard about that too. That you were all conceived during the raping of your mothers. I'm sorry about that. I'm not sure why you'd want to date me, I guess."

He laughed a little, and she smiled. It was wonderful to catch him off guard like that. And his laughter, like hers, was rusty sounding, even to her own ears. When he put out his hand, she didn't hesitate to take it with her own.

"I think that you're beautiful. Smart and fun to be around. I would imagine that you're still having nightmares about what has happened to you. I know that I would as well. But you're soldiering through it, as my boss would say. And I'd consider myself a lucky man if you were to go out to dinner with me." Before she could give it a great deal of thought, she told him that she'd enjoy that. "Great. That's wonderful. Yes, we'll have dinner tonight. Unless you have other plans."

"I don't, actually. None at all." She was embarrassed then when he kissed her hand. Cassie wasn't used to people enjoying her company. She thought that it had a great deal to do with the fact that she never allowed anyone into her life that could feel close. "I don't have a lot of clothing here. I've been borrowing clothing from the others. Their taste is a lot different than what I usually wear, but it's growing on me."

"It looks fantastic on you. I'm sure that if you were to ask them, they're enjoying sharing as well." She nodded and turned to look at the sliding door that led out onto the decking. "That would be one of my brothers. I forgot that they were coming over to update you on some things that they'd been able to find out."

It was her that got up to open the door. When Joey Phillips, another brother to Daniel, came through the door, he kissed her on the cheek and smiled. As they made their way to the kitchen, he had some vegetables that were from the greenhouse in town, she was putting them away when Joey started speaking. She stopped him before he could start.

"I don't know that I've ever thought of this before now. But could this house be bugged? I happened to think about that while in the shower this morning. How we just talk freely here." Joey laughed and asked if Daniel explained to her about his abilities. "No. I mean, are you some kind of wizard or something?"

"I can't have electronics around me. That's the reason that I don't wear a watch or have a cell phone. I can be around landlines and things that are directly plugged in but all the other stuff, it simply turns off when I enter a room. Every day I walk through the house and the bedrooms included just to switch things off if there is anything. Another reason that I keep you close is so that no one can bug you, either. I've seen that happen a few times." She asked him about televisions. "If I'm far enough away from it…most of the reason that I've never gotten into the habit of watching it, I have to be too far away to hear or see what is going on. So I've never bothered."

"That's both brilliant and sad. You can't watch things that are around. I haven't been that keen on things on television either but I've found a couple of old reruns that I'm enjoying watching. I'm sorry but also happy to know that I'm safer while around you." She kissed him on the cheek before sitting down with Joey. "What do you have to tell me, kind sir? I know that you work for the Feds. So do I."

"The president sent a few pictures to me this morning. He wants you to look them over and tell me if you recognize anyone in them." She took the handful of pictures and started sorting through them as he continued. "I have a weapon for you too. He wants to make sure that whenever you go out and are just here in the house that you're armed. He also gave permits to carry to the family that Daniel has here. The older ones, at least."

Cassie put the pictures into two groups. People that she recognized and those that she didn't. It was sad to her that she knew more of the bad guys than she did regular people. She paused on one particular picture and put it aside to finish up the others. Joey asked her about it.

"I think I know this man but not as someone that was in a wanted poster. These men I know, and while I have seen their records, I do believe that most, if not all, of them are dead." She handed him the good pile. "These I don't know at all. Should I?"

"No, you might later when and if you go back to work, but you've never had to deal with them. Wilhem told me that you were special forces with your brother. That the two of you were great at working through a hotspot without any issues." She said that she and Bradley were working for an underground group to get people out of countries that they might have burned bridges with. "Yeah, that's what he said. You've never lost a person nor —" She picked up the picture again.

"It's the driver. The one that picked Bradley and me up when we were shot. He was the man driving the van that day." She handed the photo to Daniel. "You were there too. Do you remember his face? It's the long scar that made me remember him."

"I never saw anyone but Bradley when we were in the van. Then, after we found out that you were shot, I was too busy with the both of you to look around too much. But if you say it's him, I trust you. You were in the front seat with him. Did he act odd when you got in?" She closed her eyes, thinking about the chain of events that day.

"He was annoyed that I had gotten the door open. I was thinking when I reached for the door that he was unlocking it for me but he was pushing the button down just as I got the door opened. I didn't think much of it at the time. He was also armed. The drivers are never armed when they're driving the getaway vehicle." It was Daniel who asked her why not. "They didn't want the driver to do anything else but drive the vehicle when they were picking up. Just to concentrate on getting us away, in this situation, rather than dividing their time between shooting and driving. They figured that there would be enough armed personnel in the car before...he had a Glock in his ankle holster. Also, a knife...it was lying on the dashboard with a towel-like thing over it."

She looked at Joey when he whistled. Cassie asked him what he knew. He shook his head and got up to get something out of the refrigerator. She noticed that they all did that, got into each other cabinets and refrigerators when they were over. While she wasn't used to it, she did like that they were all so comfortable with each other that they were good about stocking them so that people could feel at home.

"No one knows who he is. After dropping you and Brandley off with Daniel that day, he hung around a lot longer than anyone thought that he should have. When Wilhem showed up, the man disappeared. Along with the van too that he'd been driving. Four days later, it was found burnt on the inside with a body in the back. Without a name, it's been difficult to figure out who he is. But we're thinking, at least Wilhem and I are thinking that it was his body. His face had been smashed in as well as his hands and feet burnt too badly to get fingerprints or dental records. He's an unknown. And since you and Bradley had supposedly died, he was taken care of." She looked at the picture again, thinking about anything else that she could tell them about the man. "He had a gold tooth. It wasn't in the front but one of his eye teeth. On his right side as he was turning to me. I remember thinking, what would happen to it if he was killed."

Chapter 3

Daniel was so excited about their date tonight. It wasn't going to be all that expensive, just a local restaurant here in town that they were going to, but it was their first date, and he was happy to have someplace for them to go. He even washed the car and cleaned it up so that they'd not have to walk there.

Since Cassie, too, was living at his house with the other women and Luke, he didn't have to go all that far to get her. Just waiting in the living room with Luke while he read the newspaper. He thought it was funny that the kid enjoyed reading the daily goings on in the world. The kid was brilliant, too. When Cassie came down the long staircase with Sen right behind her, he could only stare in awe at how beautiful she looked, all dressed up.

"You look lovely." Cassie did, too. She had on a black silky dress with a beautiful slit up the side and a tiny little handbag that she told him was empty. She told him that she wasn't entirely sure what to carry in something so tiny. He laughed.

"So you're not bringing your phone so that someone might call you? Brilliant. It might not have worked anyway. I had to make sure that no one was having dinner there too, that was hooked up to a heart monitor or anything like that. You know, because of the freaky thing that happens to me when I'm around electronic equipment."

"I wouldn't have thought of that. I guess you're used to checking for things like that. Do they have a way to fix that for you?" Daniel told Cassie that he didn't want it fixed. It made for him not being recorded, not to mention he sort of liked being different. "Good thought. Yes, brilliant again. All right. I'm ready to go if you are."

The car was a great idea, he realized, when it started to sprinkle. Once they were in front of the parking lot, he let her out and pulled into the lot to park. Cassie had waited on him and he was glad for that. Having her go into a place with the shooter around that might well be gunning for her could have been just the thing that would ruin their meal, he thought with a grin. Pulling her chair out and helping her to get closer, just like his mom had taught him, Daniel sat down at his place setting and smiled. This was going to be the first of many dates, he decided.

Before ordering their meal, they were brought

out rolls and butter to munch on. He'd never been a big bread eater and was surprised when Cassie said that she wasn't either. They both ordered a vegetable platter filled with cheese and crackers as well as a plethora of raw vegetables too. They enjoyed it better than they would a salad, he thought and was glad that they were brought a refill before they ordered.

There were hometown things on the menu. There was homemade chicken pot pie, his favorite as well as meatloaf. Cassie had asked if the potatoes were real, and the woman waiting on them just tisked at her. They all three got a good laugh out of that. For dessert, there were things like cobbler, pies and cakes. And a note that claimed if you were on a diet, they wouldn't tell if you didn't. Daniel thought that was going to be his motto every time he came here to have dinner.

The dinner was fantastic. He'd always loved home-cooked meals. Since he'd had the pot pie, which he would swear was big enough for an entire family, and Cassie had the meatloaf, they were both groaning when they finished up. Since they were both sharing their food with each other, he was going to have the meatloaf the next time they came. He was told by Molly, the nice woman who waited on them, that tomorrow, if there was any left, there would be cold meatloaf sammiches. She did call them sammiches for lunch. He was both looking forward to that and not at the same time. He was just too full to think that he'd ever eat again.

Once the plates had been taken away, they sat there talking about what they had been doing before coming here, and he was glad to hear that she wanted to stay in the government jobs for as long as she could. They were still looking for the person that ordered the hits on her and her brother but for now, they were watching everyone that came around them.

"I have a pension right now that I'm being paid from. I also have insurance money too that is coming to me. The government is paying me too for the work that I'm doing for them while here. I'm enjoying it better than I think I ever did before." She told him that they were sending her cash now so that she'd have some money to use. "When people mess with your livelihood, I don't think that they think about all the issues they're messing up for you. Like having money in your accounts, your apartment, or house. When I moved here, I was lucky in that Caleb had already purchased me a house so that I could be close to them all or I don't know what I would have done. I'd been working undercover for the last sixteen months and had just ended it when I was called to help you and your brother."

"I was working for a real estate broker. Taking aerial shots of houses that they had on the market. We were watching houses to find the drug ring that was thought to be going on. However, there was plenty going on at the offices too. I've submitted my reports to Wilhem about what I'd been able to find." He could tell that something occurred to her when she looked at him. "Bradley had found something disturbing when he'd been working. He brought me in on it by showing me his laptop." She tried to think what it had been, but all she could remember was something about the doors to the house.

"Don't think too hard, or it won't come to you. That's what happens to me. The moment that I stop thinking about it, everything comes to me in a rush. Just let's talk about dessert. Do you like pies or cake for dessert?" She answered him. "I like cake too, but not as much as I like fruit pies. They're especially good when it's chilly outside, and the wind is blowing hard. With, of course, homemade ice cream."

"My parents never cooked. But we had a cook in the house that was from the south. And she cooked like that, too. Sweet tea was always in the fridge. There was always homemade bread to go with all our meals." She laughed, and he smiled back at her. "Breakfasts were her specialty. Biscuits and gravy. Fried potatoes with grits. My dad never cared for most of the things that she cooked for my brother and me, but we ate it right — we were going to meet up and go over the notes. He'd found something about a couple of houses that were drop places for drugs. Or so he thought. Just after that, he was shot. They must have had a bug planted on one of us, now that I think about it. I had been shot, too, but I didn't realize it. I had to make a call. To pick us up. That's when you were picked up as well."

"You don't think it was a drug drop?" She told him that she wasn't sure of a lot of things as they strolled around the streets as twilight was beginning to show. "Do you happen to know where the house is? I mean, we could go there and see what we can find if you think that will help you."

"He saved everything to a cloud service. Why didn't I remember that before? I guess it doesn't matter now. But we'll…I need a secure service. One that can't get out to anyone but the cloud." He told her that Joey, as well as Sebastian had them. "You think that they'll let me use it?"

"I think they'd fall all over themselves to help you out. They really like you, honey." He pulled her into his arms and held her. Whispering in her ear, Daniel told her that he loved her. He looked around to see if anything looked out of place. Now he was terrified for her safety. She looked up at him just as he was pulling away from her. "What?"

"I just thought of something." She took his hand and led the way for them to walk by the restaurant. "We'll come back for the car. I want you to...I'm not sure what you can do, but I have to talk to you privately."

As he pulled her into an alley quickly so that he could pull her into the darkness that was there, a man walked by them. Daniel was terrified, wondering how long he'd been following them. He wasn't concerned about if the man was recording him but the simple thought of him being close enough behind them made him realize that they should have taken better care when out in the open like they were. When he passed by the alley going in the opposite direction, Daniel pressed her closer to the brick wall and whispered for her to stand still.

Following the man who was headed back the way they had come, he was surprised that he entered the restaurant that they'd left. Wondering how much information the staff would tell the man about them, he slipped into the place and stood in the darkened door front. Daniel had missed the first part of the conversation but he was there in time to hear the man getting frustrated.

"They were just in here. A couple. The man is dark-haired, wearing a dark suit. A clean-shaven beard, too. Earring in his right ear." When he described Cassie, he was more worried than before. "She had on a dark dress, heels and had one of those useless purses that women carry —"

"If you got that much information about them, then how come you didn't ask them who they were? Look, they ate, paid their bill, and left. We don't take a survey when someone comes in here to eat. You should have known more about them if they were your friends, like you said." He had to laugh. Molly was getting pissed off, too, he could tell. When asked about if they used a credit card, she told him that they paid cash. "Like a normal person does. They didn't take up all my time either, asking stupid questions that I done already told you, I didn't know who they were. Go on now. I've got customers. Paying customers I gotta take care of."

The man walked right by him, not even looking to see who he was. As soon as he left, walking to the parking lot where their car was, it occurred to Daniel that he'd not seen them arrive. When he pulled out of the lot, Daniel made his way out of the building and behind it. He was going to come up to the alley that Cassie was in from that way. She met him about a quarter of the way there. Pulling her into his arms, he held her tightly against his chest as his heart started to beat a little slower.

"I should have told you this sooner, but I love you, too, Daniel. I didn't think that it would be possible again for me." He kissed the top of her head and kept his eyes out for the man. He also told her what had happened in the restaurant while he'd been in there.

"We'll leave the car here until later if that's all right with you. I'll have one of my brothers come with me, and I'll pick it up then." She told him to have one of his brothers, one that didn't have a beard to drive it home. "Good idea. Yes, I like that. I think that my heart is better now. Just…I feel really bad that I didn't even think about keeping you out of sight. I'm truly sorry for that, love."

"It's fine. I didn't think about it either. But this makes us aware that they're closer than we thought they might be." Yes, he thought that was good to know. As they made their way to the house, they both kept their eye out for anyone that they didn't know. It wasn't until they were about two blocks from their home that Tabby stopped beside them and told Cassie to get into the car.

"I'm going to walk with Daniel and you head to my house. I've been digging into things at home, so I might have some information that you might not have." As soon as Cassie got into the car and drove off, Tabby looked up at him. "You're in love with her."

"I am. I don't want anything to happen to her either." Tabby said that she didn't either. But she had some information that she was going to tell him. "Can we wait to get to your house? I don't want to have you have to repeat everything."

"Of course." As they were walking along, hand in hand in the event that someone was watching them. She talked a little about July. "She called the house earlier tonight. I guess she was having second thoughts about leaving her mother the way that she had. Beatrice hadn't been the best of parent to her and after talking to July a little, I told her not to worry about us or her mother, we'll take care of her."

~*~

Cassie was so nervous she had to ask Tabby to repeat herself several times before she finally changed the subject to talk about July Miller, not daughter but daughter-in-law to Beatrice Miller.

"Beatrice came to stay with July just after her son was murdered. Him being at the wrong place at the wrong time as it turned out. He and July had only been married for a short time. Just a little over one year. July, taking it hard that her husband had been killed by a robbery at the local quick service down the street, Beatrice had moved in for a few days and never left. After a while, July told me it just got to be easier to let her have her way rather than fight with her. July said that Beatrice had knocked her around quite a bit before she just went along. I don't know that I would have, but she told me that was only her first mistake about Beatrice." Cassie asked Tabby how she'd become to be in charge. "She didn't think that there was any money to be had from his death. It's just that July never told her about it. There was an insurance settlement as well, as she was paid nicely after the store manager of the market was directly responsible for the death of the three people in the place when he'd had it robbed. Not only did she get a great deal of money, but July also ended up with a stipend paid to her monthly from his insurance that his mother had taken out on him when he'd been a child. Beatrice took that money all for himself and lived off of July until the day she left. Even the house, which was July's before marrying Stephen, was something that Beatrice didn't know anything about."

"What was she doing coming here to claim Luke then?" Tabby explained that Beatrice thought that, like when her son had been killed, she'd get the money that July was getting from Olivia's death. "That's the only reason, then, why she came to claim Luke and Ava, the youngest two of Olivia's children? No doubt she would have tossed them aside when she got them home and the money started coming in. What about her heart attack? Had she been ill before this?"

"Yes. According to July, even before her son had been killed, Beatrice was using the power of her bad heart whenever she could. Having had four strokes during the time that she lived with July, the doctor told her that it was only a matter of time before she had one that she wasn't going to be able to blow off like she had been. She was just lucky, according to July, that she'd been someplace that had a good vascular unit so that she could have gotten good enough care that she didn't die. But as it stands right now, she's going to be hooked up to the machines that she is on now because that's the way that she wanted it. Beatrice, I mean."

"What's she going to do now that she's had a change of heart?" Tabby explained to them both. "She'll have her transported to their hometown and have her put in a home there. I guess I'd do the same thing. But I didn't care for her at all. I can't imagine how ugly it would have been living with her all this time."

"I agree." Tabby handed her a plate with a scone on it. "You're in love with Daniel, aren't you?"

"Yes, but I wish that…someone is out to end

my life, and I don't want anything to happen to him. I'm terrified that he'll take chances keeping me safe that might well get himself hurt. Or killed. But today, I thought of something. Something that might not have occurred to me if he'd not said that he loved me. Daniel said the same thing to me when he was in the van. He didn't say that so I knew, then that it had been code." Tabby asked her if she knew what the code meant. "I do now. I forgot...it doesn't matter when I remembered, but that I did. I have to go to my house and look something up. Had he not...I love him too, you see, and when I thought about Bradley saying it to me, I remembered that we had a work code. His was that he loved me. I would have said to him that I had him a gift. Those are two things, that he loved me and that I had bought him something that we wouldn't have done. Saying I love you to anyone is the same as signing a death warrant. He had something hidden at my house that he didn't want anyone to know about."

"I didn't find that you owned a home while I was digging into your life." Cassie told her that was the point, that it was a secret. "I suppose it would be really stupid to have it out there that you had a place to hide. All right. How do we get there, and when are we leaving?"

"You're not." Cassie laughed when Tabby

pouted at her. "You're too gun-ho to be out and about around where I lived. I don't want you hurt either. I'll have someone that I can trust to pick it up. The problem is that there is only one male in this household that I trust completely. I've not been around the others all that much. But I think that Toby will be in and out before I even know that she's there."

"Toby." Cassie nodded, telling Tabby that she knew Toby from her green beret days. "I only recently found out that she'd been one. I guess if you have to trust someone, it would be someone with her abilities. If I were you, and I know you're smart enough to understand this, but she should take Daniel. That way, there isn't going to be anyone recording her while around and in your home."

"I was thinking that too. Do you think that he'll do it for me?" Cassie laughed when Tabby snorted at her. "I guess that was a silly question. I'll have to talk to them both to get them set up. Christ, I don't even know where to look in my house. It's about as big as the one that you guys live in."

It took over four hours to get the plan in motion. Not alerting anyone else in the family nor in Washington as to what was going on, she gave them all the keys that they'd need to get into the place without any trouble. She was going to have to take care of her brother's things as well. But not right now. She was still hurting at his loss, and she didn't think that it would help her any to have to put his home on the market right now. It was a lovely home, one that she'd only been in once but it was enough for her to remember that her brother had loved his home as much as she did hers.

Toby dressed as a realtor was the funniest thing she'd ever seen. Not only did she have a gray wig that sported highlights like a great many women did at the age she was trying to get, but she also had on trendy glasses as well as a huge assed bag that held all the printed information that was needed to show Daniel her home. She also was armed.

Not just with her service weapon, but her glasses had a camera on them so that she could see what she saw, a Glock with several clips that were under her suit coat, and a wire, just in case, she told them. The fact that Toby was talking to herself, even before getting out of her car, made it easier for anyone listening to understand that when she was asking her questions, it was simply going to be Toby talking to herself.

Toby was going to go in first, check the house out then Daniel would come there to have a look around with the idea to see if he wanted to live there with her. As soon as her ear piece sounded that Toby was speaking to her, Cassie asked her if she could go to the big office on the main floor.

"Oh my, what an office this is. I have to remind myself to ask if the furniture stays." Cassie told her that it did unless Daniel didn't like it. "I'd take this sucker for myself if I were given the chance. This is exquisite workmanship."

"I'll let him know when you guys get back. Now, there are several volumes of smut books on the shelf on the bottom of the second bookshelf. They're by my fav author, Kathi S. Barton. Have you read anything by her? If not, then you should. The second book in the series called Aaron's Kiss, there should be a bookmark." Toby was talking about how nice the covers were and how smutty. "Yes, they are. Did you find the mark?"

"I wonder what this is? It just fell out of the book." She asked her to look at the marker so that she could tell her where to go next. Without saying a word, Toby put the marker up in front of her face, and Cassie was able to read it. She sent her to the basement to look in the wine cellar. Once she found the mark there, she sent her on several errands around the house until she collected the last one. "Christ, this is better than hunting for Christmas gifts when I was a kid. Oh, look, Daniel is here. I can't wait to show him the house."

Showing Daniel the house, they couldn't speak to each other. She had expected the fact that the earpieces wouldn't work but it still frightened her when the earpiece just suddenly cut off. Waiting two hours, that was the time limit that she was given, Cassie watched the monitors with Joey and Caleb for when they'd show up to each room. As soon as it looked like Daniel entered one of the many rooms, the camera would blip out and the screen was blank.

When the camera came back on that was watching the backyard and pool area, she felt like a huge weight had been lifted off her shoulders. Not that they were out of the woods yet, but she was happy that they were one step closer to getting things resolved to get her life back. Toby, sounding like she was speaking to herself again, said that it was great that the young man was excited about looking through the house on his own. She also, very causally, said that she had it. Hopefully, once she got the message from Toby, she'd be able to narrow down who was after her and who had killed her brother. Otherwise, she wasn't sure what she was going to do.

Daniel came back first. He said that he'd been followed to the house, but they didn't stick around. Once he parked in the long driveway, the car had moved on. It was, he thought, the same man that had followed him before. He was glad now that Harlin had gone with him. He kept him centered, and they spoke about how it was going to be the perfect house she'd heard for their brother. The two of them looked more alike than any of the other half-brothers and she was happy that they both seemed to think it was a wonderful home to live in.

Once they were back at Caleb's home, she tried to brace herself for whatever Bradley had left her. The first thing that hit her was that the note was in his handwriting. It should have been, of course, so she'd know that it was from him. However, looking at his strong handwriting, which looked like he'd taken lessons from a doctor on how to write, she brought it to her heart and held it there.

It hurt her when she thought about how she'd lost Bradley. She wasn't feeling his loss as much as she did before, of course. Nor did she think that she had quite the same kind of mental breakdown that she had when her husband had been killed. Having Daniel around, just being beside her when she held the envelope, made her feel like she could carry on. Or, at the very least, not be so hurt thinking about how he was gone and she was here all on her own without him.

"Oh, Bradley," she whispered to herself as she

opened the envelope. There were several folded sheets of paper in the bright green envelope. Taking them out, one at a time, in order of the letters on the front of each one, she had fourteen 8 x 10 sheets of paper and smaller to put together from their code. Daniel asked if he could help. "I have to start with fourteen being 'a'. Then fifteen would be 'b'. The message will be a jumble of letters and codes in these notes that I have to start with. So 'a' being fourteen, like I said, I know that the first of the sheets of paper will have fourteen numbers on them in the order that I have to decode them."

It took her nearly two hours to decide which sheet came next. Then to write down the codes inside of them. It wasn't that complicated, but it had been so long since she'd done something this way. After another six hours and some minutes, she laid them all out on the bed and read what it said. Cassie looked at Daniel with shock on her face. He was wearing the same thing on his own.

"I guess I have an idea who it is that wanted us dead. And the why of it as well. This must have taken him weeks to figure out." Daniel asked her how sure she was that he was right, nervous as she was about who it had been. "Bradley never would have sent this unless he was sure about the motive and the person."

"Well, I guess we need to make some plans to

88

get him arrested." He grinned at her. "I hope you have a better plan than I do. I just want to find a dark corner and hide out."

"I have a plan. I don't think that you're going to like it, but I do have one. It's a scenario that Bradley and I played around with when we were not working. It'll work. I know it will." He nodded and asked her what he needed to do. "I'm going to lay it all out for you in one second. Daniel Watson, will you marry me?"

Chapter 4

Their marriage, like all the others in the family, was just a filing of the paperwork that stated that the two of them had tied the knot. Daniel was happy for that. He wasn't one to shy away from the cameras, but with all the other things that were going on, he didn't want to put too much out there that might have people thinking about the long-dead FBI agent who was going to be his wife. As soon as she had asked him to marry her, he produced a ring that Caleb had given him that was part of the collection of rings that his own mother had had.

The large, beautiful sapphire was set in a Tiffany setting with small diamonds all around it. The wide band, marked with small stones in it set perfectly with the larger setting on the set. The double ring set, which also had a man's ring with it that had belonged to Caleb's great-great-grandmother had fit perfectly on Cassie's finger as if it had been sized just for her.

Abby had been given the set on her sixteenth birthday, years before she'd been raped by Howard

Berkley. As it turned out, the rings, both of them, had been much too large for Tabby's hand, and the man's ring had been too small for Caleb's own finger. He'd been set to sell them and buy something for Tabby, but he decided to share his mother's good fortune with his brothers. They all received a piece of her things as everyone had Abby to thank for their new way of life.

After things were filed away at the court house, Daniel asked for some help for them to be able to get away for a few days. At least before they were set on taking care of the man responsible for the death of Bradley Benson and the near death of Cassie. They also made the decision to not speak of it while away on the beautiful island where Tabby and Caleb had gone on their own honeymoon.

Once they were in the family's private plane, they settled in for the moderately long trip. Tabby and Caleb had made sure they were fed well on the plane as well as champagne to drink. The house they were going to be using was fully stocked as well, and the staff had gone in and aired it out, and set it up for them to use. Tabby had told them that they'd not have to leave the island for any other restaurants. Everything there was not just good but delicious as well. Also, they could easily catch their meal if it came to that. Daniel was looking forward to simply being able to not think about all the things that had been testing them of late.

"You know, I think that we're the only one of your brothers that waited until you were married before we made love." Daniel liked that as he'd been doing, she had long since started calling the other men brothers and not half like he used to do. "I'm kind of excited about this. So, let's not at all mention anything that is going on at home. All right?"

"I agree. And even if it does come up, we'll not dwell on it very much. I want this to be all about you. My wife. The love of my life and the one that has made me the happiest man in the world." She kissed him then, and he pulled her into his arms. It was awkward but fun, and he couldn't wait for them to get into more fun positions when they arrived at the house.

They spoke about going on a cruise together. And about Luke and his sisters. For now, they had plans to live in the safe house that Cassie owned as well as keeping the house that her brother had used for himself as a safe place as well. Right now, both houses were being cleaned up and repairs made. While he'd not seen Bradley's home as yet, he had fallen in love with the one that he and Cassie were going to be living in.

"I'd like to have children with you too." He asked her when. "Are you that ready to make love to me?"

"Yes, but that's not what I meant." They both laughed. "I meant, when did you want to be pregnant. I was thinking how if you were to get pregnant now, you'd have the baby in early spring, like May. However, if you wait, and I'm all right with that, you could be carrying throughout the end of summer. I've never carried a child, and I don't think that is something that I'd like to do, but I was only thinking of you."

"I never thought of the timing. Yes, I'd like a child with you whenever we get pregnant. We have a nice cool house with the one we'll move into. However, I can see where someone would be miserable in carrying a child at the end of summer if they didn't have air conditioning to bask in. Yeah, I'll have to think about that. But for now, we'll just wing it." Daniel laughed, asking her what that meant. "We'll have a child when we create one. Then, after that, we'll do the timing thing. Couple of years apart, but no more than that. I think that was why Bradley and I were so close. We were only a couple of years apart."

"All right then. That's one less thing that we'll have to discuss." Daniel settled back in the seat and closed his eyes. "I'm not tired, but my body is gearing up for vacation mode, I think. All I can think about is lying on the beach and having drinks brought to me.

Food that isn't anything that we'd have at home and the sun shining on us all the time."

He must have dozed a bit. Being shaken awake by the steward startled him. Even Cassie had fallen asleep and was having a harder time waking up. It was the first time they had slept together, she told him, and wanted to cherish it. He was still smiling when they disembarked in the bright sunlight.

Their luggage was taken straight to the house they were using. The two of them were encouraged to walk around the island to get a feel for it. It wasn't all that big of a place but it had so much in the way of beauty that it was hard not to stop at each of the places they saw. He'd been given a map from Caleb, showing where things were, like the little market and the best restaurants that he and Tabby had eaten in.

Even though they'd eaten well on the plane, they were both suddenly hungry again, and they decided to stop and eat something light to hold them over for dinner. They ended up getting lobster rolls and the island's own special drink of mango and pineapple. Daniel thought that it was slightly too sweet, but Cassie thought it was wonderful. After leaving there, the two of them walked along the sandy beach and played around in the water.

It was nearly dinner time when they reached the

house. As neither one of them had seen it before, both, especially Daniel as he'd grown up in middle class, the house was much like the house that Caleb and Tabby lived in now. Large, elegant, and wealthy.

It wasn't overdone, like a lot of the houses that they walked by on the way to this one, but it bespoke wealth on a scale that made him slightly nervous. As they headed to the kitchen to acquaint themselves with the cook who was there to prepare meals for them, Daniel had a hard time keeping to the middle of the room and not touching any of the obvious antiques that were all throughout the place. When they were shown where their bedroom was, Daniel was relieved. It looked like a regular bedroom with the biggest bed that he'd ever seen in it. Lying across the bed, he waited for Cassie to shower the sand off her feet right outside the room and join him for dinner.

After feasting on fresh fruits and seafood, the two of them made their way out to the ocean to relax. Daniel thought that he could get used to this, just relaxing and eating too much food. But he knew that it was imperative that they went back home to settle the things that were left behind when coming here. They were all in danger with things the way that they were.

Going to bed about an hour after watching the sunset, Daniel held her hand in his and told her that he loved her. Cassie told him, too, that she loved him and had decided that now was a wonderful time for them to create a child. He was both thrilled and afraid of being a father.

He'd not exactly been raised in a normal childhood. Being raised by a single mother, he didn't know the luxury of having siblings. But he was learning. Caleb and the others had made him feel just like part of the family right from the start. He couldn't have been happier about it either.

There had been trouble in his tiny family all his life. But he thought that with Cassie at his side, anything was possible. He was going to be the best that he could be and hoped that would be enough. Anything was possible, he told himself, if he had Cassie at his side for the rest of their lives.

"I want you to make love to me." He nearly fell off the bed when Cassie came out of the bathroom naked. "I think that we've waited long enough, and I don't know about you, but I'm about as needy as I've ever been. What do you think? Ready to take this marriage to the next step? Or am I being too forward?" It was the smile and the wink that got him.

"No. Christ, you're good." Stripping down to nothing but his nakedness, Daniel stroked his cock a few times as he moved from the bed and settled back on his heels where she lay down. Not only was she spread out for him, but he could smell her needs and saw her pussy soaking wet, and it was almost more than he could have imagined. It was almost too much, so Daniel touched her gently as he slid his finger into her pussy and thumbed her clit.

~*~

The climax was quick. It took her breath away and made her heart feel as if it had stopped for several seconds. It was more than she could have hoped for and not nearly enough, too. As she was trying to recover from the blast of pleasure, she cried out when he suckled her clit into his mouth. Her mind and body were his at that moment, and she loved him more than anything or anyone in her life.

Her body soared up and over without giving her any warning when she came. Daniel continued to eat at her until she thought she'd die from him making a feast of her. Even when she begged him to stop, to let her breathe, he continued to devour her. She wondered fleetingly if a person could die from so much pleasure. It was then that she decided that she didn't care. This was the stuff that dreams were made of. Having a loving husband who knew just how to pleasure her.

Cassie looked down her body and watched him look at her. Even as he slid his hands over her hips and under to her ass, her pussy felt warmed by his breath, making her more needy than she'd ever been with any other man. Cassie couldn't seem to tear her eyes from him as he continued to eat her, suckling on her clit until she nearly fainted from his loving her. When he spread her open, her thighs wide over his shoulders, she continued to watch his face. When he lifted his head, she thought for sure he was going to take her. Slam deep into her pussy and fill her.

"I want you to come again. Come hard for me so that I can get my fill of you." She nodded as her juices stained his lips and chin. It was the sexiest thing she'd ever seen. "When you come this time, I'm going to come all over this pretty pussy and make you come again."

"Yes, please. Daniel, please fuck me. I want to feel you cock inside of me. Please, I'm begging you." He stared at her for several seconds before he sat up again.

"I don't want to hurt you, but I can't resist you. My need is nearly out of control. I need you so much, love." He crawled up her body slowly, nipping at her here and licking her tiny wounds as he went. Her nipples were suckled as his cock teased her entrance. She wanted to wrap her legs around him and pull him deep but wanted to make their lovemaking last.

Forever would kill them, she knew this, but having him, just to herself, was more than she had ever hoped for in her life.

Daniel took her mouth as he entered her. He was filling her, fully and completely, to his groin, to her pussy. His tongue, tasting of her, invaded her mouth as his cock did her body. In and out, he stroked her until she knew that when he touched her sweet spot again, she was going to come.

He tore his mouth away and commanded her to come. She was so close anyway that it was no problem for her to obey him. But when she came, it was as if she came apart for a few seconds and then came back together, slamming together like she was an entirely new person.

She grabbed for something to hold onto and felt her nails dig into his chest. Blood pebbled in the tiny cuts, and she found herself wanting to taste it. Leaning up, she licked her tongue along the four tiny cuts and came again. It was something that she'd never wanted or done before. It was nearly too much and yet not enough as well.

When Daniel threw back his head and roared out, she came again, her body responding to his as if they were one. She felt his cum splash against her womb and felt his cock thicken incredibly more. She held him to her throat as he licked her ear and neck with his hot tongue. This time, she felt her vision narrow to a pinpoint before she blacked out.

Her very last thought was that this was going to be hard to top. Because she knew deep in the back of her mind that it would never be like this with any other man so long as she lived.

Cassie woke sometime in the early hours. The sun wasn't up yet, but with the purpling color of it racing across the room, she knew that it wouldn't be much longer. However, she had to get up and go to the bathroom. Stumbling a little, holding onto whatever was close, she gave herself a stern talking to about how she was going to not kill herself on her honeymoon. Nor did she want to have an unexplainable bruise on her body that someone might make a comment about. As soon as she was finished, washing her hands, Cassie looked out the window that had the ocean spread out before her.

The sun was just making itself known that it was awake and ready to take on the day when she made her way out to the chairs that they'd used last night before going to bed. However, she stood watching the antics of the ocean creatures by the shore to where she was standing.

Watching the water, she could see dolphins

leaping in the air and making her smile. As she watched, too, shrimp boats were leaving the land and setting out for their day. It made her realize how close the food that they'd had last evening had been out their door. Sitting in one of the lounge chairs after wrapping up in her robe, she sat there and was mesmerized by not just the antics of the dolphins but all the other animals that used the beach as their hunting grounds.

"Are you all right?" She smiled up at Daniel when he joined her on the deck. "I was just thinking last night that I could stay here forever, but I don't think that it would mean so much to us now if this was something that we did daily. I'm going to see about being able to rent this out from Caleb and Tabby again. I'd love to bring our children here, too."

"They'd love it. I hope they'll like the outdoors as much as we do." He sat down, telling her that they only had to make them aware of these sorts of places and would want to go back time and time again. "Yes, I can see that. The people next door to my brother's home, they had about a dozen kids. Not really, but it always seemed like that when they'd be out in the yard. But they mostly did things that were free to them. As a group, they'd go to the library. To parks to take walks. We had a feeling that they were just living paycheck to paycheck, but they certainly had a lot of adventures when the father was off for work and what we assumed were vacations."

"Do they still live next to him?" She told him that the couple had moved out of the large house when their last child graduated from high school and that they'd not seen them again. "That's too sad. I hope they get to see their kids a lot. It would really suck if they just abandoned them for the rest of their life."

"That was sort of out there. What brought that negative thought out?" He laughed, telling her that he didn't know. "Well, nip that crap in the bud. We're having fun and not thinking the worst of anyone. All right?"

"Yes, my dear." He dozed off while she watched the waters again. There was a great deal more activity going on than earlier and she had a wonderful time thinking about how the fish market must be booming about now. Waking up Daniel, she told him that she wanted to hit the market. He was up and in the shower, before she was. Cassie decided that if she were to join him, they'd never leave the place. And she wanted to see as much as she could while there.

Coming home with bags of things that they'd picked up, she was happy that the cook, Mrs. Brightly, said she'd make them some dinner with the things that they'd brought to her. There were mussels as well as shrimp that they'd been able to get, as well as beautiful cheeses with homemade crunchy bread that they could have as their salad. The vegetables were a huge hit with them both as they seemed to be able to munch on just about anything while it was in front of them. Mrs. Brightly made them up a platter of fruits and cheeses to tide them over for dinner. She couldn't believe how much she'd already eaten while here and was going to have to cut back some when they got back home.

After taking another walk, this time ending in the backyard of their home, the two of them napped off and on until Daniel received a phone call from Caleb. There was trouble at home, and they would have to cut their vacation short.

"We didn't actually enter the house before the police arrived. But I knew that there was at least one dead. The gardener had been shot once in the head from a short distance. What I was able to get to after the police went inside, most of the staff of ten were shot as well. With two of them being brought to the hospital, where they later passed." Cassie asked him about the house as Daniel put it on speakerphone for her to be able to hear. "The house has been vandalized. Most of the furniture has been destroyed. Paint had been sprayed on the walls. They told me that the word trader had been mostly what was said. No one seems to understand that, as Bradley's name wasn't on the deed."

"No. Like the other houses that we both owned, it was in a fake name under an umbrella of other companies. I don't know that Bradley even stayed there, but a few times in the last ten years. He didn't much care for the house as a whole." Caleb asked them what they wanted to do. "We'll come home like you suggested. Unless you think that's what someone wants us to do. Sort of drag us out to the forefront of what is going on."

"To be honest with you, I didn't even think of that. I was more concerned about how you guys might know what else might be going on. But yeah, you could be right on that. So I'm suggesting that you stay put. It's more than likely the best place for you right now." Daniel told Caleb not to go to the house unless the police called for you to do that. "The only reason that I was called in the first place was that their cleaning staff is the same one that I use when I need a large cleaning of the house after a party. They were trying to ascertain whether or not we'd been targeted as well."

After talking for a bit more, it was decided that they'd stay here for the duration of their honeymoon. The mood had shifted, of course, but they were determined not to allow things to ruin it all. After hanging up the phone with Caleb, Cassie called her attorney, the only person who knew that she was alive other than Daniel's family, and told him what was going on.

"Yes, I was notified about the break-in and deaths just a little while ago from the police. I'm set to go over there in an hour to make sure nothing was stolen. I don't know what it would be. I don't believe there was even a television in the place that didn't belong to the staff." She asked him about taking care of the staff's families. "They'll be well compensated. Your brother, like you, had a fat insurance policy on his entire staff as well as insurance on the house. They'll be getting about a million dollars each for what happened there. At least the family will be taken good care of. Also, I wanted to speak to you anyway about the house. It was Bradley's intention to sell the house when he retired. I believe that he was setting things up so that he could. Did he mention that to you?"

"He did. He had been saying that for years, but I think that the last time we spoke about it, he was more set on retiring than before. Do you think I should have it put on the market? I was actually thinking about living in it rather than the one that I have. It's much larger and will be more updated than mine will be when we can move in." He said that was what he was going to suggest. "All right. Then have the place fully updated to this century. Also, while you're at it, have mine done at the same time. That way, we can get as much as we can out of it."

"Very good. I'll have them started on as soon as the police are finished with Bradley's home. Yours I'll have started on today." She thanked him. "I will also send out some photographs of the second house that I have. Nothing about the murders. But it will show you and your new husband a—I'm so proud of you, honey. You've no idea how happy I am that you found yourself someone when you needed them."

"Thank you so much, Henry. I love him so very much." She nearly warned him about the things that were going to come out soon but decided that he'd have to wait like the rest of the world. And the world would be decidedly shocked by it all as well. "I'll speak to you again when I get back home. Thank you for doing this." After hanging up with her attorney and friend, she asked Daniel what he was thinking about. He looked like he'd been thinking hard about something.

"Just wondering what will happen when this all hits the newspapers. It will, you know? It'll hit the papers in Ohio first, then after that, everyone will have a piece of it. And have an opinion on it, no doubt about that." She wondered if he had one, and he just grinned at her. "I do, but I think that it mirrors yours. It has to be done, and with all the shit that has gone down with it, it needs to be done sooner rather than later. It's been too long as it is."

"I agree." She stretched out, hurting in a couple of places that she'd forgotten about, and told him that she was going to figure this out before it got too close to the time. "I want to get DNA tests done on myself as well. But we'll have to be sneaky about it. Like figuring out who else might be in on this thing."

"I don't know how you can do that without involving the entire family. I know that they'll help, but you'd have to explain to them why your brother was targeted and why you thought that you were shot at as well." Cassie told him that she thought that it might be because Bradley might have told her. "That's what I'm thinking too. Even though he did tell me later, I never would have guessed it. Not even when we were alone had he ever mentioned it. I think that he hadn't any idea that he was his father until right before he was murdered."

Bradley had found out, quite by accident, that he wasn't the son of their father. That his mother, like Daniels, had been raped and conceived a child. Bradley. She was curious too to find out if she'd been another child conceived that way, so that was why she was having a DNA test done on herself. It boggled her mind that someone would do that once to a person, much less twice. She was going to have the tests done as soon as they returned home. She was also going to do this on her own, without the family expediting it for her to get results. That would be a red flag that would get them all into hot water. And more than likely killed.

The next few days found them talking more and more about the murder of her brother. It actually felt good to have someone to talk to about him. Daniel was a great listener and she enjoyed his input about what might happen when it came out. He also told her that he was worried about Caleb and how he'd take the news about it all. His mom had been directly involved in getting Wilhelm to run for the presidency, and she didn't want anything to happen that would tarnish her good works and name. As they were headed home, she felt relieved to be getting this over with. There was a great deal at stake, but she thought that it was the best thing for everyone involved.

Getting home, they took a nap. They hadn't been doing all that much, it seemed but they would make love then fall into a deep sleep that wasn't all that restful. She thought it was because they had so much on their minds that they couldn't relax enough. Even for as much sex as they were having, it didn't seem to matter when they went to bed. They were still exhausted throughout the day.

Applying for the DNA test, she was thrilled that Joey, one of Daniel's brothers, was able to do it for her so that no one would know who it was from. As soon as the tests came back, they were going to do what should have been done sooner. Confront the president about having her brother killed and raping her mother. This shit was going to end his career if it didn't put him in prison for the rest of his life.

Chapter 5

Wilhem was looking forward to sneaking off to see Caleb and his family in a couple of days. Keeping up appearances had been his specialty since he'd been a kid. He would laugh his ass off when he was able to pull the wool over someone's eyes. And it was especially wonderful that he had fooled Abby for so long. Then she'd gotten smarter. Or stupider. It was her fault that she'd had to die so soon.

He had hated to kill her off. Not that she ever used her money to further his campaign, but he knew that when he ran again, Caleb would be there for him. Killing Abby, or having her killed, was the most brilliant move he'd ever made to date. Now not only did he have the ear of the richest man in the world, he had him fooled as well.

It was the only way that he could keep his secret, killing Abby. How she found out was beyond him, but having one of the people working for him slipping into the house and feeding her poison was his best idea to date. She'd had no idea that she wasn't dying of cancer.

Having doctors in his pocket and nurses, too, had made it easier than he'd thought. Then, convincing her son, a sap, if there ever was one to have her cremated and her ashes with him, he knew that he'd covered all his bases. Christ, he was brilliant, he told himself all the time.

Checking his calendar once again to make sure that he had it there and nothing else, Wilhem decided that he might have to leave a little earlier than they had planned for him. It was going to be wonderful to talk to them and show his sorrow for the loss of someone so special. However, he was going to hit up Caleb about helping him out when he was ready to put his name on the ticket again. Things were looking up.

Glancing at his cell phone when it rang, he smiled. Caleb again. The man thought that he had it all. Well, that was for now. He was going to take as much as he could from the idiot before he decided that he'd drained him dry enough. He'd been thinking about telling him that he'd been thinking about having him as his running mate when his next term came around.

His mother had always told him to keep your enemies close to you so that you could make sure that they were not going behind your back. He wasn't sure that she had been saying that correctly but it had worked for him for so long that now he wanted to make it his next campaign slogan. However, he wasn't sure that would go over all that well. But he could think it, he told himself with a chuckle.

"Hello, my dear boy. How are the plans for me coming around to see you and your family?" The silence at the other end of the phone had him looking at the phone to see if he'd lost connection. When he could see that it was indeed still connected, he nearly said something more when he felt something at the back of his head. "Caleb? What's going on?"

"You've fucked with the wrong family." He asked him what he was talking about. "The gun at the back of your head should be enough to let you know that I'm not as simple as you seem to think I am. Nor was my mother."

Dread washed over his body. He felt his face pale, his body tense up for whatever was said next. As he tried to regain control of himself and not say anything that would get him into more trouble than he seemed to be in, he took in a deep breath and was careful with his next words.

"I'm afraid that I don't know what you're talking about. You'll have to…why do you feel it necessary to have me held at gunpoint? Explain yourself before I have you arrested." Caleb laughed. However Wilhem thought that had he been standing next the other man, he might well have noticed that it wasn't humor that was making him laugh but anger. "What's this all about?"

"The man behind you has instructions to kill you if you so much as move in a way that he doesn't like. In about ten seconds, less more than likely, there will be a news crew in your offices with the police and secret service." He heard the door open behind him and didn't have to look to see. They were surrounding him in a way that he could see them. "Now, the news crew is going to record what is going on. Also, you'll be thrilled to know too that my mom's death is being looked into as we speak. Your suggestion or demand that she wanted to be cremated was a lie, too. You've become so good at lying all the time that I'm sure that you can't remember the truth any longer."

"I still have no idea what has brought this on." A sheets of paper were put in front of him. It took him a few minutes to figure out what it was he was looking at. "I don't know where you got this from, but there is no way that I am the father of Bradley Benson."

"Oh, but you are. Right in front of you is not only the truth of it all but that you were also the step-brother of Howard Berkley, the bastard that got away with the things that he did to so many women. And if you turn to the next page, you'll see that you are also the father of Cassie Blake Watson." He closed his eyes and thought about what this was going to do to his career. "You raped Mildred Benson several times over the years while she worked in your household, and it resulted in the two children that she raised on her own. The very least that you could have done was support her. But I guess that you'd not be able to run for the presidency if you had a murdering stepbrother as well as several illegitimate children running around. I don't know how you pulled the wool over my mother's eyes, but you're going to pay now."

"And how do you think that it going to be proven? Do you think that coming in here and threatening me with a gun to my head is going to be overlooked by the public? It's not. And so you know, I'm not going to allow you do anything that will jeopardize my chances as the — to think that I was going to ask you to be my running mate." The pop to the back of his head hurt, but he didn't turn. Whoever was behind him had the advantage right now, so he was going to pay nicely. For now. "Why don't you come here like a man and talk this over with me. Tell me what you think that you know."

"I know quite a bit. I know that you killed my mother. That you — " He told him that she had died of cancer. "No, that's what you wished for us to believe.

But the nurses that you hired to kill her have confessed to you blackmailing them. Shut up while I tell you what I know for a fact. I know that you're the one that killed Bradley Benson. That you had a hand, a large part in the near-death of Cassie. That…there is so much that I'm going to have you tried for that it's going to take the courts a very long time to get through. You're finished. As of right now, you'll never see the light of day again."

"What are you going to do, Caleb? Kill me? I won't believe that. You don't have the balls for that. You Mandy-pandy asshole. You and your mother were saps. And you want to know what else? Nothing is going to harm me. I'm a well-loved president. I've done this country good by being here in the White House. Who do you think the public is going to believe? You or me?"

"Are you saying that I'm not smart enough to cover all my bases? I've done my homework. So did my mother. I believe, in some way, she even knew that you had her killed off. Why? What did she ever do to you that had you killing her off?" He told him. In great detail, how much he'd wanted her dead, so did it. "She was the kindest person that ever lived, and you murdered her."

"Yes, I did. And I'm going to kill you, too, as

soon as I can get there. You'd better have all your ducks in a row, Caleb, I'm coming for you." The gun to the back of his head dug deeper into his skull. Wilhelm had forgotten about the people in the room. His anger was so out of control. Laughing a little, he asked Caleb if he thought that he'd done anything to bring him down. He had to do something to cover his own tracks here. Then, a thought popped into his head. "You're insane. I've always heard that it's best to agree with an insane person. That's what I was doing. Agreeing with you until I can have you locked up."

"Sure you were." His temper was getting the better of him and he had to pause for a few minutes to make his head stop pounding. "The man behind you has instructions to make sure that you don't do anything stupid. I know that is likely something that you strive to do, but try not to piss him off. He's a very good friend of the family, and I'd hate to see him get blood on his hands because of you." Wilhem glanced behind him and turned back. "I see by the look on your face that you know who he is. Good. That way, I don't have to introduce you to him."

"You're in with the mob, are you, Caleb? My good Christ. Is there nothing that you won't do to get a few bucks?" He asked him why he thought that he needed money. "Why else would you be here? But to blackmail the president of the United States. Surely, you can't believe a word that has been coming out of your mouth. You moron, this isn't going to get you anywhere but dead."

"No, I don't think so." When he didn't say anything else, he asked him what that was supposed to mean. "I'm not going to be dead over what I've done to you today. I think the American public will be thrilled to know that you've been caught. I know that I'll sleep better at night by knowing that you're gone."

"What do you mean, gone? I'm not going anywhere. And if you think that you're going to be able to get out of here with me, then you're in for a rude awakening, Caleb. As it is now, you're stretching my patience. I'm this close to having someone go to your home and have you arrested." There was a shuffle behind him then a chair was put beside his. Before he could guess what was going on, Caleb was sitting in the chair next to him. Like they might well have been at his home enjoying a nice conversation. "What is this supposed to prove?"

"Tell them to arrest me. Go ahead. See how far your demands work on the very men that were supposed to protect you." He was almost afraid to tell the men around the room to arrest Caleb. He had a feeling that they wouldn't do shit for him now. Not even take a bullet for him. "Too afraid, are you? Well, because you won't do it, I'll tell you flat out. They won't lift a finger to help you."

Pissed off, he turned around in his seat and looked at the people that had come into the room. It was not just the secret service men, at least a dozen of them, but also three news crews recording him on their cell phones, Caleb's wife as well as the rest of the family. Then he noticed that his Vice president was there as well as the speaker of the house. Christ, he was in deep shit here if he didn't figure out a way to turn things around.

"I can see your mind working right now. What can I do? What can I do to make this go away? Nothing. You're well and truly caught with your drawers down around your ankles, as my mom was so fond of saying. You remember her, don't you? The woman that was my mother and the woman that you murdered?" Wilhem told him he was a liar. "Am I? Well, I do have this that was taken just yesterday when I had her body exhumed."

"She was cremated. There is no...you were to cremate her. I told you that's what she wanted." Caleb asked him why he'd believe his word over his own mother, telling him that she wanted to be buried. "Christ, Caleb, have you any idea how all this is going to affect me? Why are you doing this to me?"

"A better question would be to ask yourself, why did you do all of this? Why kill these people? My mom. Your child. There are others, too, that we're looking into. The two men who shot and killed Bradley. Their bodies have been located. It's funny that. It's almost as if they didn't trust you when you told them you'd pay them well. They both, separately, left a long confession and who had hired them to kill the two Bensons. Also, one of them had a recording, with your voice verifying what you wanted done and how you wanted no witnesses. I guess they didn't realize—or perhaps they did that by no witnesses meant them as well." Wilhem didn't know what to do. He needed time to think. He was usually good at thinking in a jam, being able to get himself out of anything so long as he had time to plan. But right now, with all this going on around him, he couldn't think past the fact that he was in deep shit. "Something else you need to be aware of, you're not going to go to prison. But you will be dealt with."

"What's that supposed to mean? You're not going to kill me. Or have me killed. I'm a very powerful man, and I can't just disappear. People will ask questions." He nearly jumped out of his skin when someone knocked a book off of a shelf. The room burst into laughter when he cried out and put his hands over his head. When he was ready to knock some heads around, he noticed that there was a large screened television being plugged in. "What's the meaning of this now? Are you going to watch cartoons? I heard that you were just immature enough that you sat around watching them instead of working."

He told himself that he wasn't grasping at straws here. Even when the words slid from his mouth, he couldn't believe them himself. No one said a word but no one was looking at him either. Turning to look at what everyone seemed to be glued to, he saw himself as he hadn't.

There sat an old man who was past his prime and sitting in a chair that was much too large for him. It took him a few minutes to realize that it was him looking back at himself. Even his suit, one of his favorites, looked as if he had some of his lunch on it as well as his tie looked like he'd used it for a napkin, it was so crumpled up.

"Am I on television?" He looked around the room and realized that he wasn't in a good position to be talking to the American people. "What have you done to me? I demand that you turn this off and—"

"The people want to know if it's true that you had one of your own men killed and nearly killed one more." He asked his aid, a man that he'd been meaning to fire for some time now, what he was talking about. "You've been on the news since it broke that you were being taken from office and arrested. The American public wants to know if what you've been saying is true. Though I'm here to tell you that I don't think they'll believe you anyway."

"What is the meaning of all this?" Smiling at the camera that had been in the room all this time. "You've caught me at a disadvantage, I'm afraid. I usually have something prepared when I speak to the public."

"You mean the truth of what the others have been accusing you of? Or is it the lies that have spilled from your own mouth when you speak about how you're going to protect us? I guess we should have been wondering if you were protecting your own butt and not those who put you into office." He couldn't think beyond the old man staring at him from the screen in front of him. "Mr. Davis, are you listening to me?"

Wilhem stood up and sat down again quickly when he saw one of his agents, *his agents* put their hand in their gun. This was getting out of hand quickly, he thought. Standing up one more time, he stood there thinking, his hands on the desk that he'd come to love so very much. He asked if there was any way that he could have a few minutes on his own to take care of some things.

Given five minutes, he made his way to the door but was cut off. He was pointed to a chair that was just off camera, and he sat there. Christ, he was going to prison. Or someplace no one would hear from him again, that was for sure. Putting his head between his knees, he reached down to tie his shoes. From there it was an easy thing for him to pull out his small revolver and put it to his chin.

~*~

Daniel had to laugh each time he thought of Davis and his attempt at suicide. The idiot actually thought that he could get off that easily when there were several men around who were ready for him to do something stupid. He'd not come out completely unscathed, having his arm broken when he'd been tossed to the floor like a rag doll had made it so that he got to treat him. Daniel hadn't even bothered with giving him anything for pain. In his mind, he didn't deserve any kind of niceties after all the shit that he'd done.

"You're thinking about Davis again, aren't you?" He turned to look at Cassie and smiled. "Yes, well, I don't know if you have gotten this far yet, but everyone in the entire world wants to speak to you. Why, you ask? Because Caleb told them that this was all our plan to bring him down."

"Well, it was indirectly." She smacked him on

the arm. "We got justice for your brother and you. That more than makes up for everyone wanting to have an interview with us, don't you think? Also, you won't have to be looking over your shoulder for the rest of your life. And you can come out of hiding. Not that you were really hiding away, but it's nice to be able to move around the town now."

"Yes. You're right about that. I'm also happy that he has to face judgment, too. Or has the powers that be decided on something else for his punishment?" He told her that everyone wanted him to face the jury of his peers. "Good. I think I like that better. Everyone should hear it from his mouth about the things that he did. By the way, how is Caleb doing today? Yesterday, when I spoke to him, he was still upset about things. I wish we'd been able to tell him that Davis killed his mother before that day. My heart breaks for him."

"Mine too. She was directly responsible for all of us being found, and it hurts me, too, that she's not here to meet us all. I think that's his feelings as well." He thought of Caleb after the televised thing with Davis. "His heart was broken. I don't know what he might have done had he not had Tabby there for him."

They all, his brothers, had gathered at his home to be with Caleb the morning after Davis was taken away in cuffs. He had been sitting at the dining room table going over the books that his mother had put together about their lives. Each of them had taken a book when they arrived and had asked questions about the trip or adventure, which in turn got Caleb to talk about her more. Then, the unthinkable had happened.

Last night, Sheppard Anderson, grandfather to Caleb and dad to his mom, passed away gently while taking a nap before dinner. His uncle, Shep, had been visiting and when his dad drifted off, he'd gone into the kitchen with his mom. They'd only been gone a few minutes, and when they returned, he was already gone. Melissa, his grandma, had taken it very hard, and Daniel had sedated her so that she could be calmer. It was Shep who had called Caleb and he was so broken that it had been difficult for him to say the words.

"Did you hear that Melissa was going to be living with Caleb and Tabby? I think that it won't be long before she joins her husband. Shep said that she was taking it pretty hard herself." Cassie asked him if he knew her all that well. "Not really. However, the others did. I was the last to arrive so I didn't get to spend as much time with her as the others. Sheppard was a good man, and I really enjoyed speaking to him."

"I didn't know either of them but only in passing. It breaks my heart too that Caleb has lost so many people in his life." Daniel agreed with her too about Melissa. He was going to make sure that he spent some time with her as a doctor and friend. She didn't need to be thinking of joining her husband just yet. "How much longer before our house is ready? I think you were talking to the contractor when I came down this morning."

"I was. He said that it would be at least another week. The paint is dried but the carpet needs to be taken up in two more rooms. He said that it was so old and dirty that it would have to be taken up with masks and the whole nine yards." She nodded and told him that she loved him. "And I love you. More than I can put into words."

He knew that he'd spoken to Caleb and Tabby about signing the other house over to Sen and her family. It was going to be a good home for the five of them and large enough, too, that they could stay in it and raise their own families. They were close, the lot of them, and he couldn't think of a better way to stay together than for them to live in such a large home together. Plus, they got to see Luke whenever they wanted. He was becoming a fixture in all the homes in the family, and he believed like they had done, he had his own room in each of the houses that he could stay in.

When he opened his eyes, not even realizing

that he'd dozed off, Cassie was just sitting down in the lounger. Asking her where she'd been, she told him that they had an offer on the other house. Intrigued, he sat up in his seat and asked her how much.

"Well over the asking price. In fact, just as you predicted, there is a bidding war going on between four couples. I think that our asking price was a good one but with the way that this is going, we're going to end up with double that we had marketed it for." He rubbed his hands together and laughed. "You're silly. But what do you think we should do about this? Let it go or accept—hold on. I have another message. We have another bid on it. Ten thousand more than the last offer."

"In answer to your question, I think that we should just let it ride. If they're willing to pay that much for it, then we shouldn't burst their bubble." He laughed when she did. "I think the money will go a long way in doing the things that we wanted to do when we talked about it. Since you're willing to share your insurance money with me and everything else that you have, I'm willing to help you spend it."

"Again, you're silly." He was also being paid by the government for his part in the arrest of Wilhelm Davis. While he didn't have any idea how much that would be, Caleb said it would be a good deal of money.

He'd also explained that whatever he had, they all had, but it would be nice to have enough money in the bank to at least come and go as they pleased on trips. They were both retiring from the Feds, but he was going to remain a doctor in good standing until he couldn't do it anymore. It was the one thing that he'd done that had made his mother proud of him. And he was going to do it just for her. If for no other reason than she was his mom, and he loved her.

The evenings were shorter, the sun going down a good deal sooner than he wanted it to. Daniel still tried to cram into a day more than he should have, but he was able to sleep at night and not wake up aching because he'd overdone it again. Getting to sleep with his best friend helped, too. Cassie and he were as close as anyone else in the family.

"What do you say that the two of us take the kids, I'm betting now that it would only be Luke up to Amish country and have a day of it. I know that Mrs. B has been wanting us to head up there for a while now. Something about the best cheese prices in the world." He said that he wasn't entirely sure that they were the best prices, but he'd love to go. "I have to go into town in the morning. When I get back, we'll head out. You see if Luke or any of the others want to hang out with us."

"I'm betting that we're going to have to get us a larger car if they all say that they want to go. I'd rather not arrive in a limo if it's all right with you. I don't know why, but I think that would draw more attention than arriving in a buggy." She laughed and went into the house to get herself a smallish—he had no idea what that was blanket that she could use. Pulling out his cell phone, he called the house.

After asking if any of them wanted to go with them, he knew that the van rental for the day was going to happen. After getting the women to calm down, squealing about the fun they'd have, he was glad that they decided to drive up themselves if he and Cassie would travel with Luke. After hanging up, he called his other brothers and their wives to find out if they wanted to go or needed for them to pick up anything. The consensus was that the prices were hard to beat on a great many items that they were going to see about picking up for the others. Also, and he thought this a wonderful idea since they were leaving in the morning to do their shopping, the others, including Caleb and Tabby were going to meet them at one of the restaurants to have dinner together.

Daniel was in bed by midnight. Luke had decided to come and stay with them so he'd be ready. He said that the girls, his sisters, would hog up the bathrooms, even though they each had their own, and he'd be without hot water. Or he'd be in hot water. He couldn't remember which he'd said. Laughing a little he crawled into bed and wrapped his body tightly around Cassie's. She'd gone up to bed earlier and was now fast asleep. He didn't blame her for sneaking off. He was simply too exhausted to make love to her again tonight.

When his phone rang at a little after three, he was pulling on his clothing even as he took messages on what was going on at the hospital. He hadn't been on call, not his turn, but he took the call anyway. It was a delivery of one of the Johnson families. There were three of them in town with two of them having a baby soon. Daniel was out the door before he could remember that he had plans for the morning. Well, he was going to make it happen even if he had to make a few calls himself. His family came first and he wasn't going to let them be disappointed if he could help it.

Chapter 6

Chase knew that Daniel was pissed off, but so was he. Since the man was already at the hospital and working, why did he think that he should come in? He had plans today as well and it didn't involve the hospital where stinky people were and nurses making demands on him. He didn't even know why he'd answered the phone. But seeing Daniel's smiling face made him think that it was a social call and not him being called into work.

"You're on call, Chase, and I'm not. The very fact that they tried to reach you and you didn't bother answering makes me think that this job might not be for you." He rolled his eyes, telling Daniel that he liked the money it paid. "You're not going to be paid at all if you don't do your job and come to work. You do know that I can have your pay docked for this. And I'm going to make sure that you're docked for all the other times that you didn't show up for work. Have you even worked a weekend when you were on call?"

"Yeah, yeah, I know that I've been remiss in

working when I'm supposed to, but I have to have some downtime, Daniel. But as for today? I have plans with my family. You see, I have this big assed boat that I just got, and I'm going to go out with my family. Plus, my wife and I are having a bit of trouble around here. You understand that, don't you, buddy?" Daniel said that he didn't and had plans as well and that he wasn't his buddy. "But you're already at the hospital. It would be silly if I were to come in now, don't you think? I mean, you're already dressed for the job and everything."

Linda, his wife, pointed at her wrist and started tapping her foot. He'd never understood why people still did that, pretending like they were showing you a watch when people hadn't worn watches in a decade or more. He certainly didn't. Chase remembered someone had commented on that, too, that he needed to have a watch on because he wasn't to have his phone out all the time. Stupid rules if you asked him.

"Look, you get your ass in here right now, and I won't have to bring you up before the board. This is the fourth time that you've blown off being on call, and the other doctors are getting sick of covering for you. You have thirty minutes, or you'll be regretting your decision to stay at home." No he wouldn't and told Daniel that. "I'll have you fired, Chase. I'm not kidding right now."

"You can't fire me, Daniel, and we both know that. We're short-staffed as it is. I only came on board with this hospital because of the bonus I'm to get in a few days." He counted it up and smiled. "Three days, Daniel. I'll have that five-grand bonus in just three days. You can hang on until then. It's not going to be all that busy. I can feel it in my bones."

Chase realized that he was talking to a dead receiver when the sound came through. Calling him an asshole for just hanging up on him, he looked at his pissed-off wife. Standing up, he was thrilled beyond words that he wasn't going to have to go to work. Delivering babies was something that he never wanted to do, but it came with the job. Christ, he hated holding onto a wiggly squiggly baby and all the nasty shit that came with one.

They were nearly packed up to be gone. Spending the day on the boat they'd just gotten was better any day than staying in a smelly hospital when he pulled out of the garage to load up the beer and coolers that they'd gotten yesterday when the boat arrived. But he couldn't leave because he'd been blocked in by the police, of all things.

"Officer? What is it I can do for you?" His wife asked him what he'd done now, and after telling her that he'd not done anything that he could be arrested for, she went into the house. Good, he thought, he could tell her anything that he wanted when they left. "Is there something going on that—"

"We're here to take you to work, Doctor Slate." He asked if he was joking. "No, sir. Daniel called and said that you were having trouble coming into work, and we told him that we'd help you out. So if you'd like to just get whatever you need to have—"

"You have got to be kidding me. He actually called the police on me because I didn't come to work today? Like I tried to explain to him, I have plans. He's already there. It would be stupid if we both had to ruin our days off to—"

"Are you on call or not, Doctor Slate?" He said that he was. Thinking he could get out of this right now, he reached for one of the many beer cans that he'd yet to put into his truck. "You touch that, and I'm going to have to arrest you. Daniel is a good man and has plans, too. He wasn't even on call today. You are. Now, I'm going to ask you again to step back from the beer that you have there and get into the cruiser with me. I don't want to have to arrest you. And I'm sure that is nothing you want either."

"What are you arresting me for? I mean, he doesn't have that much pull that he can have the police here to take me in. Does he know that if you take me in, I'm still not going to be working today anyway? I bet he never thought that far ahead, has he?" Chase reached for the beer, not thinking about the threat that had just been told to him.

Getting the tab pulled on the can, he had it to his lips, ready for his second swallow, when he was suddenly on his stomach lying across the hood of his truck. No easy feat either since the sucker was a good three feet from the ground. When his arms were jerked behind him, he asked what the fuck was going on. It wasn't until he heard the racking of a rifle that he turned to look at his wife.

"Now honey, there is no need for you to be pointing that thing at the nice officer." She told him to shut the fuck up. "It's just a small misunderstanding right now, and I'm going to have it all cleared up in no time."

"You fucking bastard. You told me that today was our day and that you were off. Fuck, Chase, do you ever tell the truth anymore? Oh, and your fuck buddy or whatever you call your girlfriend, she's is on the phone." He didn't think that this day could get any worse than it was right now. "I want him out of here, officer. If it helps, he's been drinking since seven-thirty this morning and hasn't stopped. I believe it's against the law to be drinking on the job."

"Yes, ma'am, it is." After being read his rights, Chase asked if he went to work could he just call this a misunderstanding. "You're drinking. I doubt that you're drunk, being how you have been drinking all your life, but I'm going to test you. It's against the law for you to be drinking on your job. I'm betting that you lose your doctoring license for this. Yes, I do."

No amount of begging got him out of the situation that he was in. Chase even begged to talk to Daniel, telling them that it was just a misunderstanding and that he'd make sure that Daniel understood that. As he was tossed, Christ, they didn't even try to keep him from banging his head on the car frame. He was told to shut up and enjoy the ride. Like that was going to happen.

When he was processed and put into a cell, he decided that he needed to talk to Daniel. The man was a sap, sure, but he'd see that it was just a misunderstanding and have him drop the charges. He didn't know how that was going to work, but it was worth it. He decided to use his one call to contact the man and see what he could do for him. It was worth a shot, and he was willing to bet that the dumbass would fall for it. He had gone to work when he wasn't on call.

He didn't answer. Christ, the man was really

starting to piss him off. Trying to get him to the phone was proving to be more difficult than it had been to convince the salesman at the boat dealership that he made two hundred grand a year. Chase wondered if there was going to be an end to this fuckery that was plaguing him right now.

Leaving a message seemed beneath him, but he had to try. "Hey, Daniel, buddy. I'm in a bit of trouble here and was wondering if you'd come down here and talk to these officers about how you and I had a deal or something? I'll leave the details up to you, you're a smart guy and all." He nearly gagged, thinking about how much he was buttering the guy up right then. "Anyway, I need your help with this. I don't want to be in jail. Hey. You can use my boat anytime you want to. You know, so long as I'm not using it. And never on weekends. Also, you'll have to put your own g—"

Being cut off pissed him off more, and he slammed the phone down. He was so pissed right now that he wanted to break something. Before he could get the chance to toss the phone across the room, he thought that if Daniel didn't come through, he should call himself a lawyer. Just as he was looking up one on his phone, it was jerked out of his hand and put into a bag.

"What the fuck are you doing? I have to find

me a lawyer." The man, a guy with a flak vest on, told him that he'd made his call. "No. No, you have that all wrong. He didn't answer. I left a message, so that doesn't count as a call."

"Did you say you left a message?" Chase told him that he had, as Daniel must have been busy or something. "Counts as a call. Come on, Mr. Slate. It's time for you to go to processing. You need to empty your pockets. I'll have your phone but with the rest of your things."

"It's Doctor, not Mister. I'd appreciate it if you would address me as such. I worked hard for that title, and I want you to use it."

He'd not worked all that hard for anything in his life and being a doctor had been easy when he'd cheated on everything that the school had tossed at him. Even going so far as to hire someone to take his boards. Life was just too easy for him at times, and damned Daniel was fucking things up for him.

Taken back to his cell, he was pissed off again when they told him that he'd missed breakfast and that he'd have to wait for lunch. Since it was almost nine in the morning and the fact that he'd skipped breakfast in favor of having a couple of beers, he knew that he was going to be starving if he didn't get something soon. What he wouldn't have given for just a couple of beers right now.

~*~

"Let me guess, dumbass, Slate didn't show up for work again." Daniel laughed even though his temper was on edge. He'd called one of the other doctors to see if they could come in. "Or was he drunk on the job? I wouldn't put either one past him at this point."

"Both, I guess. He didn't show up and actually told the service that he'd traded with me and that I was the one on call. Also, I sent the police to pick him up to bring him in, and the fucker had already been drinking since he'd gotten up." Something occurred to Daniel just then. "Has he been drunk showing up to work?"

"I don't know that I'd call him drunk. I think that his tolerance is a bit more than mine would be after a couple of drinks, but yeah, he'd been drinking when on the job. I think he has a real problem, that boy. You had him arrested, did you?" He told Doctor Lance what had happened. "That's great. Oh, how I wish I'd seen that. I bet the little pecker was trying his best to get a deal made too. The shits that are coming out of college nowadays... Well, it makes me want to rattle their brains a bit. What did you need? I'll come in for you if that's what you want. Having Chase arrested has made my whole day, hell, maybe my whole week."

"My wife and family and I had a plan to go

up to Amish country this morning. Eat some dinner there, too. If you'd not mind, you'd save me a lot of heartache. We're taking Luke Branch and his sisters up with us, too." David told him that his wife had been wanting to go up there, too, before the holidays. "I can pick anything up for you if you need it. It'll be my pleasure for covering for me today."

"Nah, but I thank you. I think she wants to go for the shopping. Cheese is just something that she wants me to think that's all she wants. My wife. I love her to bits, but I think she has it in her head that I'm not so bright." They both laughed, and Daniel thanked him again. "No problem, Daniel. I'll be in by nine...I was going to say nine-thirty, but it's about that now. I will be in before ten. I think my wife wants me out from under her feet anyway. This will be good for us."

"Thanks so much, David. I'll make it up to you. I promise." He told him that he'd already done that by having the dumbass arrested. "That was the easy part. He did that all on his own."

True to his word, David was coming through the doors at five until ten. Shaking his hand, he told him that he'd seen his wife in the parking lot and for him to get going. Telling the man thanks again, Daniel briefed him on the woman who had come in that wasn't in labor. Daniel had set her up in one of the rooms to rest, and he was out the door and on his way to having fun before David could change his mind. Kissing his wife, they were on the road to having fun.

The day was perfect for an outing. Daniel was able to take Luke to watch as the cheese was being made, making the youngster's day with it. They did buy their weight in cheese, he thought and had a wonderful time tasting the things that they were buying.

Pleading exhaustion from having to get up so early for Chase, he sat down on one of the benches to take a little nap. However, when Sen sat down next to him, he could tell that she wanted to talk to him about something. Smiling at her, he asked her what was going on.

"You always seem to know. I mean, when one of us comes to you— Never mind. I know you wanted to take a nap here, but this is important. It's about the house." He asked her if she needed repairs or something. "No, nothing like that. It's about the rooms that we have. I'd like to...I'm going to college with Luke this fall. It's going to be a lot for him, but having the house and seemingly unlimited foods brought by the rest of the family, we were wondering if you'd allow us to give someone else a chance that you've given us. Giving them a room while in college."

"Do you have someone in mind?" She told

him that she didn't but she had seen a lot of people struggling that may well drop out. "You'll have to have them looked into. I'm sorry to say this, but there are people out there who would take advantage of your offer and never leave. I've read about squatters a great deal in the paper."

"So has Luke." She laughed. "He is the one that brought this up. But he was nervous about coming to you about it because you think of him as a kid. I know that he is, and so does he, but he has the soul of an old man. I don't know if you've noticed that about him or not."

"I have, as a matter of fact." He thought about it and decided that he'd have to start treating them all like adults. Not so much Luke, he was extremely smart, but he was still only ten years old. "I think that it's an excellent idea, but you should run it by Caleb. It's not up to him, but with him having big bucks, I'd say that he might well have run into this sort of situation before. Giving people a hand up. He'll know the things that you guys would have to look out for more than I would. I'm sorry that I don't have an answer for you."

"You did. And I appreciate you not just shutting me down. I think that others might well have. I'll talk to Caleb and tell him that you're on board with it if he is. I also wanted to talk to him about some investments that my mom had." Nodding, she kissed him on the cheek. Daniel asked her what that was for, not that he didn't like it. "For everything that you've done for us. Also the million and one things that you've done that we don't even know about. Thank you seems too small in comparison, but I want you to know that we appreciate you and Cassie a great deal."

When she left him there, sitting in the shade on one of the most comfortable chairs that he'd sat on in the outdoors, he decided that he could always sleep. Spending time with his family and extended family on limited time. Also, he was going to buy several of these chairs to put on the deck. He could see him and Cassie taking naps in them when they were old and gray.

Finding Cassie wasn't that difficult. She and the other women were sitting on the same chairs kind of chairs that he'd been in, eating raw vegetables. Thinking that was a very woman thing to do, he didn't mention it. He might be silly at times, but he wasn't stupid. Women could be and would be just as mean as any man he'd ever encountered.

Taking a couple of pieces of celery, he asked them what they were going to be up to now. It was Luke who answered, telling him that they were headed to the all-year Christmas shop down the road. After telling Cassie what he'd done, she kissed him on the cheek as well. Daniel thought that he could get used to this, hanging out with a group of women.

"Can I stick with you from now on? I love my sisters, but I'm running out of patience with them." He nearly laughed but just caught himself. Daniel asked the little man what they'd been doing. "It's still five months until my birthday, and they're looking at things that I'd like to have in my room. I don't want anything in my room, Daniel. If there is a lot of stuff in there, it's going to distract me from studying. I don't mind a picture of all of us, but I don't think I'd like to have my room decked out like I'm some kind of cowboy."

Again, the urge to laugh nearly had him coughing but he looked away and wiped at the tears that were forming because he didn't fall into the humor that was strangling him. He spotted a couple of places that he thought Luke would enjoy and decided that he'd guide him there. Who didn't like to be in a candy shop with someone willing to foot the bill?

Daniel thought that he'd ended up very well upon leaving the candy store. He was also sure that he'd spent more on himself and Cassie than Luke did on him and his sisters. They were both carrying large bags and filled to the brim with tasting what they didn't know when they met up with the others.

"We have one more shop to hit." He asked her

how many times they'd been to the car, only joking because he was thinking of taking their purchase there. When Cassie told him, with a beautiful blush on her face, he couldn't be mad at her even if he tried. "We'll be all right. I might have to take a loan out to cover it all, but I think the girls are enjoying this very much."

"And you are as well. Yes, we'll be just fine, honey. You go ahead and spend as much as you want." He hoped that she didn't take that as a challenge when they headed off to the row of stores where the candy shop was. "Well, Luke. What's it going to be now? Do you want to go and see what kind of trouble we can get into down the road? There are several drink places that I'd like to go into. I'm in the mood for a smoothie."

Luke was more than glad to get himself a drink, too, and sit at one of the tables to drink his drink. They also, because why not, decided to open a couple of the candy bars that they'd gotten and have a quick snack.

"Sen told me that I need to eat more vegetables. I told her that I would if she did. Now she's on this kick that all of us have to eat more of them. I don't mind a salad, but if that's just the meal, I'm gonna die. I'm a growing boy and need to have meat so I can grow big and strong." This time, Daniel didn't hold back but laughed. "Sen is dating this guy who I think is not good enough for her. I mean, I know she's an adult and all but this guy seems more like he enjoys showing off his muscles and not using the one on his head. Before you tell me, I know that the brain isn't a muscle, but he doesn't use it at all. Sen said that I would never think a man is good enough for his sister. She is kinda right on that, but she doesn't have to date the first dummy head that asks her out."

He supposed things like this would come up for the kid, and since he was surrounded by females most of the time, he'd need to voice his concerns with someone, too, who wasn't related to him. Thinking of the right things to say to him, Daniel took his time sipping his drink.

"Does he hurt her? I mean, you said that he is proud of his muscles. I would hate to think that he'd hurt her to, I don't know, prove he's stronger than her?" Luke said he'd not thought of that, then stared at him. Daniel knew that he was thinking about it. The boy wouldn't say anything until he was sure. However, he did tell him that he didn't want him to think of it if the guy was nice. "You know, she's been wearing a lot of makeup. Even around the house. Also, and I just thought of this, when we're having family time, she's been wearing her long-sleeved sweaters."

"Luke, it could be nothing at all." He nodded, but he could tell that he was worried about it. "I'm sorry if I upset you, buddy. When Sen spoke to me earlier, she didn't mention it. And I have no idea why, but I think she would have if it was bad, don't you think?"

"Why? My momma didn't." He had a point. "I had to take these classes once when it talked about how sometimes women will go for the same person their daddy was. Like if their dad, like ours, was beating her all the time, then that's the sort of person that she'd find. Like it's all right or something. It's not. But she might think that way. Don't you think?"

"I don't know Sen that well yet. But I would hope that she'd ask for help if she needed it." Daniel tried to think if Sen had been wincing at all. If she had a habit of covering something up on her body. Not once did he remember her doing anything like that. "What are you going to do, Luke? You're going to have to handle this delicately."

"No, I'm not. I'm going to straight up ask her." He pulled out his new cell phone and dialed her. "You might want to prepare yourself, Daniel. I'm thinking that if I'm wrong, then she's going to be hell-bent for leather, as my mom used to say."

Daniel finished his drink. Looking around for a place where Luke could talk to his sister privately, he heard him talking. Apparently, she wasn't all that upset with him, and no, Lester wasn't beating up on her.

"You'd leave him if he did, right? You don't have to go in the same footsteps as Mom did, are you?" She must have assured him that he was right because he leaned his head on the table, and he could hear him sniffling. "Sen, I don't have all that much in the world, but you, my sisters, are the best. You'd tell me, wouldn't you? Or someone? Right?"

A few minutes later, Luke closed the connection, but he didn't move off the table. Daniel asked him if he was all right. Luke, instead of telling him that everything was fine, he told him that he didn't believe Sen.

"All right. You know her better than most people. What makes you think that she's lying to you? You have to have a better answer than just staying that you think she is." He said that he didn't know. "Has she lied to you before? I mean, on something important?" Luke sat up, and Daniel could see his tears.

"I don't know, but I'm worried. If she will lie to me about this. Do you think that I'm wrong?" Daniel again said that he didn't know, but he could ask Cassie to look into things for them. "I'd like that. But she'd have to be careful. Sen really does like Cassie, and I would hate to ruin their friendship because I'm being a dope."

"I'll talk to Cassie as soon as we meet up again. She's been with her a lot and might be able to point out things that you wouldn't see." He asked because he was so close to his sister. "Yes, that's part of it. The rest is that you've known her all your life, and she might be perfectly fine, and so is this Lester person. If it…no, we don't want to go down that road."

"You mean asking one of the others to look into his background? Yeah, I thought of that too. That would really have Sen blowing a gasket. And that sucker would rain down on me. Nah, not going to go down that road like you said." The two of them got up to do some more walking. He didn't want to tie up the seats anymore than he had already. As they were entering the next shop on his list, a big building that said that it had something for everyone, it seemed that Luke wasn't thinking about it. At least not as hard as he'd been earlier. Daniel was going to have to watch what he said to Luke. He was a very protective brother and it didn't matter how old or big he was either.

By the time they made it to the restaurant, he really did need a nap. Everyone else looked like they did as well. However, when the rest of the clan showed up, it was a while before they were seated. Lucky for them, Tabby had called ahead and told them that they needed a lot of tables and they even gave them a room of their own to enjoy.

"I'm going to have fried chicken until I cluck." Everyone laughed at Luke, and it embarrassed the kid a little. "That's all we heard about when we were walking around. Like how good the fried chicken is and the mashed potatoes. I hope they don't run out."

"I'm going to have some of that silk pie they were giving away samples of in one of the shops." Cassie winked at him. "And I'm going to have it before I get too full to enjoy it. Anyone game for having dessert first?"

As much as he wanted to have his dessert first, Daniel knew that he couldn't eat one more bite of sweet treats. He thought right then that he had made a huge error in having gone into the place before dinner. But, he also told himself he was going to be clucking too if it came to what he was going to have. Caleb told him that he'd not eaten lunch to save up room for this meal.

He didn't have the heart to tell him that it didn't work that way. Instead, when the staff came by to take their drink order, he ordered unsweet tea for both him and Cassie. He was going to cut calories everywhere that he could. At least where the drinks were concerned.

It took him ten minutes of simply walking around the buffet table to figure out what he wanted to start on. Watching his brothers, he could see that they were going for the chicken. There was plenty of that in the bin so he wanted to try something that he'd been wanting in some time. French fries and mac and cheese.

"Oh yeah, you're watching what you put in your mouth." He grinned at Martin and told him that at least his stuff wasn't fried. After that, it was like a challenge had been laid out. Just to see who could eat the most and not explode before going home. He didn't care if he won or not but thoroughly enjoyed the play between the lot of them.

Chapter 7

Cassie was going to make sure that the next time they wanted to spend the day walking around shops, she had a scooter of some kind. Smiling to herself, she helped Daniel put some of the things that they'd gotten into the large pantry. It was one of the deciding factors in them using her brother's house over the one that she'd had.

"I'm going to go up and run you a bath. Then I'm going to join you because my body has this idea that it's been run over by several women trying to get to the sale items." He looked pointily at her. "Know anyone's footprints that might match the ones on my back?"

"I told you a dozen times that I was sorry. And I didn't run up your back like I heard you tell Harlin. I simply shoved you out of the way when I heard what they were having on the special. You'll thank me in the morning when someone makes you French toast on that cinnamon swirl bread." He told her that he'd gladly be her leapboard whenever and wherever she needed him to be. "Thank you, I think. Now, tell me what you've been wanting to talk to me about all day?"

"Okay. Luke is afraid that Sen is being abused by her big-muscled boyfriend." She said yes. "Yes, what? He is? If so, you'll have to visit me in prison."

"He only hit her the one time—" He started to cut her off, and she put up her hand. "I know that once is enough but it had been an accident. He'd been trying to open one of those tabby kind of soups for her, and the lid came off faster than he thought and since she was standing there at the time, he socked her in the face. I believe her if that is what you're going to ask me. He took her to the emergency room and had her fill out a report on what happened. He even called the police in so that they could hear what had happened to Sen and begged them not to tell anyone of the men in this family. That's why she's been using makeup. That's why he bought her about three dozen roses since it happened and the reason that she didn't tell Luke the truth. It wasn't really a lie but a form of protection for Lester. I guess he was so terrified that one of you might jump to conclusions that he had Sen meet his mom, and apparently, she is part of an abusive relationship that one of her own brothers had to step in and make right."

"You're sure that's all it is?" She told him that

she was. And that she told Sen that she'd make sure that everyone, even her brother, now that it's out, that she knows better than to stay in a relationship that you have to hide from. I swear, I believe every word that she said. "Thank you for that. I also wanted to talk to you about Luke. I'd like for him to stay here or with one of the other men a few more times a week. The kid is seriously lacking in male companionship."

"I can get on board with that. By the way, I'm seriously lacking in male companionship as well. How about we go upstairs, and I undress you? We can have a night of debauchery if you want." He nearly knocked her down, pulling her out of the pantry they were in to drag her upstairs. Laughing, she told him that there was plenty of time.

"No, there's not, I'm afraid. As soon as I hit my pillow, I'm going to be out. I know this, so if we don't start now, I'll be out before I can get you naked." Cassie told him that she was going to get him naked first. "I love that idea. I love you, Cassie Watson. With all my heart."

They went up the stairs slower. Cassie did wonder at some point if Daniel was up for this but he assured her that he was. To prove his point to her, he pulled her into his arms and kissed her. The man was devasting when he wanted to be, she thought with a grin. Christ, she might have bitten off more than she could chew.

Once they were in the bedroom, she told him to stand still. Pulling his shirt out from his pants, she unbuttoned it, careful not to touch him too hard, but she did flutter her fingers over his hot skin as much as she could. Getting to his belt, something that she hadn't noticed until then that he wore one with jeans, she did the buckle, and then watching his face, she pulled the leather strap one loop at a time, pausing at each one to breathe on his nipples.

"You're beautiful to me." Daniel seemed to struggle with words when she spoke to him. He said that he loved her. "Oh, Daniel, I love you so much. I struggle with the words to tell you."

Dropping the belt to the floor, she put her hands on the buttons on his pants. She knew that the button-fly jeans were coming back in style, but right then, she wished that they weren't. Undaunted by the five silver snaps, she pulled the first one free. When she had an idea, she looked up at Daniel and asked him if he trusted her.

"With all that I am and then some." He grinned at her then. "Don't hurt me, Cassie. I don't want to die before I see my firstborn." She looked up at him.

"How did you know?" He asked her if she

knew what he did for a living. "Yes. I guess I didn't figure you'd be...I'm going to have your baby, Daniel. I nearly called you right then at the doctor's office to tell you. But I thought you'd pamper me too much, and I'd not get to have fun today."

"I'd never...well, I would love to pamper you, but I like my balls right where they are. But you don't want to—Holy good god, Cassie."

Kneeling down in front of him, she put her mouth over the next snap and opened it. It was much easier than she'd thought it would be, and did the next three that way. However, she ran into a block, his thickening cock when the last one was too tight to get open.

Instead of having him do it and take her fun away in the process, she licked along his heavily veined shaft before freeing his cock. It was like she'd freed it just for her mouth. As soon as Daniel begged for her to stop before he came, Cassie pulled his boxers down over his cock and ran her tongue over the dark crown.

She hadn't expected it to be so tasty having a man's cock in her mouth. His cum was there for her to sample, and she found herself swallowing as much of his precum as she could. When he pulled his pants down to his thighs, Cassie followed him to the side of the bed, still licking and suckling at him while he sat down.

With his pants off, she had so much more room to explore. She didn't close her eyes but watched his face as he'd done to her when he'd been eating her. Thinking about how much she had enjoyed him tasting her, she stood up, stripped down, and got onto the bed with him. Her pussy to his mouth and his cock at hers.

More and more of his cum slid down the back of her throat and along his delicious cock. It made for easy strokes for him by putting her hand around him and fuck him with her hand. When he reached between them and tweaking at her nipples, she felt a wave of something, a climax that she'd not expected had her crying out.

"Come again, love. I love the taste of you." Cassie only nodded, not caring if he could see her or not. Right now, she was going to make him come all over her if it was the last thing she did tonight.

Moving her body around so that she was on top of him, still with his cock in her mouth, she rode his mouth like he was riding hers. There was no more gentleness from her, and she didn't think that Daniel was slowing down either. As soon as he stiffened beneath her, she knew that she was in for the rush of her life.

His hot cum touched her on the face, her hair,

and her breasts. Lifting up just a bit more, grinding her pussy into his mouth, she screamed, feeling her throat burn with it when her own climax slammed into her. Like her entire body was being flipped up and over several times before she was able to come a second time, then a next. All the while, she felt her body giving all it had. She never stopped making love to his cock with her mouth.

The sudden flip to her back had her nearly crying out again. When Daniel moved over her, pussy to cock, he slammed into her so hard that she felt it at the back of her throat. The next time she came, it was too much, and her body simply gave up trying to keep up with him. Darkness took her under quicker than she could close her eyes.

She must have been out for a few minutes because when she opened her eyes, or eye, one of them was still on strike, she was at the top of the bed on her pillow and a sheet drawn up over her. Daniel was just coming out of the bathroom when she sat up.

"Don't touch me." She had to laugh at the desperation of his voice. "I'm serious right now. You touch me, and I'm not going to be responsible for what happens to me. Right now I feel like I could spin off in space, never to return." She laughed as he got into the bed, staying as far away from her as he could. "I don't know what got into you, but give me fair warning next time. I think perhaps I'm never going to be the same. And if we have that sort of making love again, we're going to test the fact that I'm a young, healthy man who should be in a fit enough state to have sex."

Cassie laughed off and on throughout the rest of the morning and into the afternoon. After lying next to Daniel for about another hour, she got up, showered down the hall so as not to disturb him, and headed out. There was a great deal for her to get done today, and she didn't want to sit around waiting for her sore body — yes, she thought, it was sore to catch up with her mindset on the list she had to get done.

Her top-of-the-list thing was to make sure that the rest of the family got their packages sorted out from the ones they had brought home in their car. Everyone had pitched in where they could, putting things in every car or truck so that they'd not be overly crowded driving home after an exhausting day of fun. While she was out, she was stopped by no less than ten people asking what was going to happen to the old high school now that the new one was being built.

"I don't know about the things going with the high school." Just to make sure she drove by the ancient building just to make sure that there was nothing going on there. Nothing that she could see.

"When I get home, I'll ask then and let you know. But right now, I've no idea if there are plans to renovate it or not."

Getting some questions answered about the two buildings in the downtown area that were earmarked for projects, she could tell that construction was working on them. It had been Caleb's idea to use the locals for smaller projects and to hire a construction team for the larger ones. The renovations for the library, as well as the new roof on the courthouse, were being worked on, she could see but the school project brothered her. Just as she was pulling out her cell phone to make a call, it rang.

"I need your help." It took her a second to figure out that it was Sen. "Can you please come and get me. Also, I'd appreciate it if you weren't to tell anyone. This is going to be bad when it hits the fan."

"I'm on my way." She started to ask her what was going on but didn't want to know so that she'd not drive like an idiot and get herself hurt. She was pulling up in front of the big house when Sen came out of it with a large hand towel pressed to her face with what appeared to be blood. As soon as she got in the car, she told her to go to the ER.

"All right, but if this was Lester, his ass is going to prison. If he lives that long." She said it was his father. That she needed to find Lester and let him know what had happened. "What did happen?"

Before she could tell her if she was going to, they were pulling up in front of the hospital. After being briefly seen, Sen was taken back to a room. Not taking no for an answer, she followed her back to the room and sat down next to her while the nurse and a doctor examined her cheek. The cut to it looked like it had been made by a knife but it was hard to tell from where she was sitting. When they left to prep her for stitches, Cassie asked her who she needed to call.

"Lester. Then, if you can't get in touch with him, and I'm going to be so freaked out if you can't, then call the men in. I believe that his father might have hurt him too." She asked what happened, and she started crying, babbling about how she'd not seen it coming and that it hurt her heart that— "I think that Bill, Lester's stepfather, killed his wife. He kept saying something about her not being worth anything to him now that there was fresh blood in the family. I didn't think about it until I laughed at him that he was off his meds. I don't know that he was on meds. It's just…Is it all right with you if you call in Daniel? I love you like a mother, but Daniel is like a father figure to me, too, and I need him here?"

"No, I'm not upset with that at all. He has a

calmness about him that… Honey, I'll call him now."
Stepping out into the hall, she called him. Cassie was
so happy that he was awake and out and about that,
she asked him to meet her at the hospital. After giving
him a brief rundown as to what happened, he said that
he was on his way. She told him not to tell his brothers.

"I'm afraid it's too late for that, honey. The police
showed up at our house when Caleb and Martin were
there. They're pissed off, as I'm sure that you know."
She told him to make sure that they were calm before
driving in. "I'm very calm. Pissed as I've ever been but
relatively calm too."

She didn't believe him and was glad when he
said that of the three of them, he was the calmest.
Cassie was afraid that the women would find out what
happened then there would be hell to pay.

~*~

Daniel stayed with Lester while he was being
examined at the emergency room. He could have
treated the younger man but he was asked to keep him
calm. Having to hold the man's hand throughout the
examination and ultimate cast put on his leg as well as
his arm, he told him that he should get the stitches put
in his face so that it would heal better. Daniel thought
it was very telling that he didn't want anyone to see
the stitches or they'd get the wrong idea.

"And what idea was that, Lester? That your stepfather is a bastard. People are going to be very helpful to you from now on." He asked him how he thought that Serenity would take it, glad that he was calling Sen by her full name. "She's had to have a few stitches put in her cheek as well. Doug cut her because he was hoping that you'd not want her again so that he could take her. Did he ever show this kind of behavior before?"

"No. Not even when I wasn't around. At least that's what...are you sure that he killed her? I mean, she does have a bad heart. Could she have died... She was supposed to have a long life now that they'd found out what was wrong with her, and she took things easy. I just don't want to think about her suffering at his hands, I guess." Hugging the kid when he started sobbing, it hurt his own heart to think of the suffering that Milly had suffered before dying. "She's all I had in the world, you know? My mom was everything to me. Then Serenity came along, and I felt like...I love her, Doc. Serenity is everything to me. And now she's been hurt by that fucking bastard, and I'm going to lose her. I don't know what I'm going to do."

"You're going to buck up here and tell her how sorry you were. Not that I think you have anything to be sorry for. You took her to meet your family, and the bastard showed his true colors." He gave a brief thought to what he would say to the other man and decided that he was old enough for the truth. "Your mother has been examined by the staff, and she's been hurt as recently as the last few weeks. The examiner said that she had years of new breaks and bruises on her body that happened in the last few months."

"She didn't tell me. Why?" Luke, who had been lying on the bed next to Lester since he'd brought him in, was finally asleep. He'd been stressed about the young man and was glad that there seemed to be a bond forming between them that they both needed. Thinking about what Lester had said, Daniel said that he didn't know her at all, so he couldn't make that judgment. "Mom told me once that she'd made a mistake in getting married again. I thought she just meant that she missed her freedom. I should have looked into it more when she was alone with him."

"She'd gotten used to hiding herself away from others finding out. I would imagine that it was difficult, too, for her to admit that she'd made another mistake in finding herself caught in an abusive situation again. As I said, I didn't know her but I think I might well have thought the same thing." When his cell phone rang, he saw that it was Cassie.

Stepping outside to take the call, terrified of the

news that she might have, he leaned against the wall when she told him that Sen was in surgery and was expected to make a full recovery. After telling her what Lester had told him, the two of them cried a little for the things that the young couple had gone through.

"He told me that he loves her." Cassie said that Sen had told her the same thing about him. "I hope they can get through this together. Who is with you guys now? Hopefully, her sisters. Luke has been lying on the bed with Lester, holding onto him. I think he fell asleep about ten minutes ago. Apparently, he loves the man too."

"Good. They need something positive in their lives for a change. I like this man, Daniel. I don't know what is going to come back on his background or even if there has been one made, but I hope the two of them can work this out, as you said. I think they'll need each other to get through this. And having a good man in their family is something that they all need." He agreed with her and then asked if she'd heard anything about Doug. She said so far as she knew that he'd been arrested, and that was all. "That's good news. I think that everyone will rest easier knowing that he's not out looking for them. We'll keep each other informed about what we hear. Caleb and the others are making funeral arrangements for Milly. These two aren't going to be fit to do it anytime soon, I don't think."

When he went back into Lester's room, the nurse was just finishing up giving him something for pain. In addition to having a nice-sized cut on his face, one on the cheek and the other on his lip, he also had a broken leg as well as a few broken ribs. He'll be down for a while, the nurse told him, as they were going to take him to surgery in a little while, and this was just to take the edge off his pain.

"The little one, he won't be able to go, mores the pity. I think the little guy here is good for Lester. He's been a lot calmer since he's been in here with him. You too, doc, but that boy there, I think he's about as much in love with Lester as his sister is." She asked him how she knew that. "The young lady has been making sure that he is getting the best of care down the hall. When the surgery is over for the two of them, we're going to put them in the same room. I think they'll both heal a good deal better than worrying about each other.

Daniel picked up Luke and wasn't surprised when he woke up suddenly with fists flying. After getting him calmed down a little, and hugging him when he started crying. When he was assured that Lester was going to be all right, he settled him in the other bed so that he could sleep. Again, Daniel was responsible for holding someone's hand, and he couldn't have been happier.

The two surgeries went well. After having their bones set, the two of them were put into a larger room together. As soon as Sen woke up, she asked about Lester and was glad to see that he was in the same room with her. Since little Luke couldn't get into bed with them so soon after surgery, he was glad to be able to sit on the chair between them and keep an eye on them both. The others, all his family and Sen's came in and out of the room to sit with them as well. It was nearly daylight when Lester woke and asked after Sen.

"I would like your permission to ask her to marry me." He started to tell him that it wasn't up to him when he dozed off again. Over the next couple of hours, he asked him again and again, telling him each time that he loved Serenity with all his being. At just after nine in the morning, the police showed up to talk to the couple but left when it was obvious that neither one of them was fit to have a coherent conversation. Daniel was happy for that. He thought that it would be terrible timing, with the two of them still in a great deal of pain, to ask anyone for anything right now.

"They're going to both go home with the daughters. That was the plan anyway. However, I asked, with you being a doctor, if they could stay with us while recuperating. I don't know what you think about it but I do think they'll be pestered less with the sisters around all the time if they're with us. I can imagine that they'd be hovering over them all the time. Can't you?" He agreed, saying that while he was sure that they meant well, it wouldn't help with their healing. "That's exactly what I thought, too. Luke wants to stay with us. I think he'd be better off doing that, too. He's never been so worried about anyone as he seems to be the two of them. I have a feeling that it's not going to be long before they're married and have their own family. What do you think?"

"He told me several times that he wanted my permission to ask her. At first, I wasn't sure why he'd think that I had anything to do with him asking but he told me later that Sen had thought of me as her father figure that she's never had. I believe we're about the same age, so I wasn't sure how to take that. But I did give him permission and am glad that I did." She asked him if she would want a big wedding. "I don't think that she'd want that but I have a feeling that her sisters will want to be bridesmaids for her. They might be a little pissed off if they can't get all dressed up. Lester asked me to give her away already. I believe she's going to ask you to be her matron of honor, too. We might even be asked to be grandparents to their children."

"That's wonderful." He held her to his chest as they sat on their couch. The house was coming along well. They'd moved in a couple of days ago while the last of the renovations were going on. The house that Cassie had had was sold now and they'd gotten much more money than they'd thought they would. He remembered something that he'd been meaning to tell her for a few days. "I heard from the CIA. The ex-president has been put into a deep hole. I'm not sure if that's a literal term or not, but they swear that we'll never have to worry about him again."

When she didn't answer him, he realized that she'd fallen asleep, and he smiled a little. It wasn't often that the two of them could nap anymore. Today was special. They had the entire house to themselves, and he was glad that they didn't have any plans for the evening. It seemed that they'd been running full out since they'd met. Having something normal, like sitting on the couch in their own home, was something that he'd been missing. Closing his eyes, he was nearly asleep when he felt a presence in the room.

Opening his eyes and looking at Luke, he could tell the little man had been crying. Putting out his free arm, he was happy that he didn't say anything but crawled up on his other side and snuggled with them. Daniel couldn't have been happier than he was at the moment.

"Luke?" He answered the whispered question just the way that he'd asked him. "I wondered if it would be all right if I called you dad. I've never had a nice one before, and I really like Lester, but...well, he's going to be my brother. So I'd like to call you Dad."

"I'd be honored, Luke, but you should maybe talk this over with your sisters." He said that he had and that Sen said that she thought he needed a father figure. "I believe you do as well. Do you think that Lester would fit the bill?"

"No. I mean, he's all right, and I really like him, but no, I want you to be my dad. You see, we have this thing coming up at school where we have to bring in our fathers to look around the college with me. Moms can come too, but the professor said that it would be a good bonding time for the two of us. Even though I'm not going to be living on campus for a while yet, I'm taking classes online until I'm a little older. They said that I should know the buildings so that if I have to come in, which I will for testing, then I'd have a good idea where I was going." He told him that he'd love to help him out with that. "Good. And I really do want you to adopt me, Dad. I'll be a good big brother to your own kids, too."

"If I adopt you, which I'm thinking that I will if

Cassie is all right with adopting you too, then you'll be my child as much as the one that we're having too." It took Luke a moment, but he sat up and looked at him, then at Cassie. "Yes, she's going to have a baby. Don't tell anyone yet. We're going to keep it a secret for as long as we can. And being our son, you should know too."

The rest of the evening after Cassie woke up was making plans for the holidays. Halloween was coming up quickly, and Caleb had decided to make a huge deal of it. He didn't know what that entailed, but he was just as excited to participate as the rest of them were. It was going to be epic. He knew to have such a wonderful family getting together as one. Yes, he thought, it was going to be the best holiday he'd ever had. And he was looking forward to it with all his heart.

Chapter 8

Daniel waited as patiently as he could for word on the birth of his newest grandchild. It had been six years since the wedding of the century, as it was being called by anyone that had been invited, and Sen and Lester were the happiest couple he'd ever seen. They still acted like they were in a honeymoon mood and loved each other like they had hit the lottery every day of their life. He loved it.

"How many grandkids do you have, Daniel? I know it's a bit more than Tabby and I have." He had to stop and think a moment but it didn't slow Caleb down in talking to him. He noticed that nerves made him do that. "I still can't believe that you adopted Sen and the rest of her sisters when they were in their twenties. You were about their age, weren't you?"

"Yes. Sen is actually only a few months younger than I am. And Alex is the same age as Cassie. When they asked me if I would, I thought they'd been joking. But they made the courthouse appointment for us, and I did it. It's wonderful having so many children that really don't need you as much as someone younger might." He shook his head. "No, that's not right. They needed me more than I think a younger child would need me. Plus, I've eleven grandchildren that are the same age as my two are. I couldn't ask for a better family than the ones I have. You and all my brothers and all my sons and daughters. I think, however, that I'd like to have a granddaughter. Having all those little boys—and big boys is nice, but Cassie and I want to see just one little girl in this family."

"I know what you mean. I have four daughters. To be honest with you, I think I'd be happier with little boys. They can't be hurt by men like us when they start to date." Daniel laughed and said that he was nuts if he thought that men could be any less hurt. "Yes, I guess so. See? That's another reason that I'd like to have a son. Just so we can hang out together and do manly stuff."

Daniel snorted at his brother and told him he was lame. "At what point did you ever do manly things? You don't even plant the flowers around your house." He said that he watered them. "You have a system hooked up that all you have to do is push a button. Christ, man, your button-pushing finger gets more exercise than you do."

"What do you do that's so manly?" Daniel told

him that he'd never said he was manly. He had. "All right then, tell me what you did yesterday, mister smarty pants."

"Yesterday, when the swing set arrived for the backyard, I put it together. I have learned, too, that reading the instructions is a vital part of putting something together. My wife taught me that." Caleb said that instructions were for pussies. "Yes, for you, perhaps, but not for this guy. I love it when I only have to put something together—how many times did you have to put together and take apart the new grill you got? I think before we left to go and get something to eat, you'd done it about ten times."

"Bullshit. It was only six. And I finally got it together, didn't I?" He cocked a brow at Caleb and just stared him down. "All right, I didn't get it put together, but Tabby did in only about twenty minutes. I'd been at it for six hours. It works really nicely. I'll have to have you guys over again, but this time, there will be food."

"Are you planning on cooking again?" Caleb said that it had only been the one time that he'd burnt the roast. "Yes, but how many times have you burnt the popcorn? Or, for that matter, made your kids some powdered drink and 'accidentally' used salt instead of sugar? Three times that I know of. How can you fuck that up so many times? It makes me wonder if you don't need to go and get your eyes examined soon."

He was saved by Lester coming out of the delivery area with scrubs on still. All of them stood up to wait for the information that he was about to tell them. From the grin on the man's face, he was sure that everything had gone well.

"We have a son." He laughed. "And two daughters. Everyone is healthy, Serenity is doing great, and we're parents to triples. They're the most beautiful babies I've ever seen."

He came to him and hugged him. Daniel could tell that he was crying, but he'd bet his life that he was both overwhelmed and happy at the same time. He knew that he would be as well. When he pulled away, he grabbed him again and told him that he loved him so much.

"And I, you, son. You've been a great son-in-law and a better man than anyone I've come across. Thank you for taking such good care of my little girl." They both laughed, and he asked if they had names yet. "I mean, you did know that you were having triples, I'm assuming."

"Twins. We thought we were having twins. Even the doctor was surprised when the girls were born one right after the other." Patting him on the back and wiping away his own tears, Daniel asked if he could see Sen. "Yeah. She was sleeping when I left her, but she told me to bring you in right away with Luke. Did he make it here?"

"He's on his way." He thought about the young man who was going to run for the presidency after serving as governor of Ohio within the next decade. There was no doubt that he'd do it too. Right now he was studying to get a doctorate in the law because he wanted to be prepared when he hit the White House. For a sixteen year old, he had his life pretty much mapped out better than he ever had. "Did he tell you that he's going to be taking on a large case? I still see him as that little boy that was in need of male companionship, and here he is driving and going to one of the most sought-after colleges in the nation."

As if he'd summoned him to them, Luke showed up and hugged everyone. As they made their way back to Sen's room, Luke was telling them how traffic had been backed up for miles because of an accident on the highway.

"However, it didn't appear to have any fatalities at least. Just a lot of banged up people that were standing alongside of the road." Daniel told him not to mention that to his sister, or she'd be wanting to go to the ER and help out. "Don't you know it? Getting her nursing degree had made her the happiest but she doesn't take that many breaks."

All of the Branch girls, well now they were all for the most part married, had gone into some kind of medical field. He'd never been more proud of anyone than he'd been at them. Daniel entered Sen's room and noticed that she was still sleeping. However, the babies were there, and he couldn't help but to peek in on the three of them.

"You can hold her." He grinned at Sen when she struggled to sit up in bed. Daniel knew better than to offer her his help. They were still independent and would murder you in your own bed if you offered to help anyone of them. "We've not named one of the girls yet. And as you suggested, we didn't name either one of them Abby. I think there are enough in this family as it is."

"Yes, I think that we all have at least one child named after her." Daniel picked up one of the girls and handed her to Sen when she asked. After Luke had a seat, he handed him the other girl, and he sat down with the little boy. "My goodness, young man, you're going to be a heartbreaker. Look at all that hair you have already."

Stripping the baby down to his bare skin except for his diaper, Daniel counted his fingers and toes. Also, because he couldn't break the habit of being a doctor even though he had been retired for a little while now, he checked his heart and lungs. When looking at the child's face, it looked as if he was fully aware that he'd not been ooh and awing over him but giving him a full workup.

"When will Mom be back? It seems like she's been gone forever, and I know it's only been a couple of days." He told her that she was on her way home now. That the assignment was over on this case. "I'm so proud of her for doing what she does for the government. I've seen some of her videos online. I know that I can't tell anyone that it's her, but I'm very proud of her."

"I am as well. However, I think this is the last one that she's doing. She's sick of missing out on important events." Luke said that the baby he had had pooped. "Well? Change her. I know you know how to do it."

"Gross, no, I'm not changing her diaper. Yuck. I might get it on my hands or something." He took his sister's baby and handed her the dirty diapered one. "You do it. She's your kid."

Daniel took the little girl and changed her himself. Also, doing a thorough examination of her, he was happy that she was as healthy as her brother had been. Once he had her snapped into her clothing again, he took the other child and changed her, too.

"You're going to have to tell them when they're older that you checked them out after the doctors and nurses did it. They'll think it's funny that grandda had to make sure that they weren't duds." He kissed Sen on her forehead before taking the little boy back and holding him. "I love you, dad. I always have."

"And I love you too. After their time was up, the staff saying that Sen needed her rest, he remembered to take their pictures. Lying them side by side, he took about ten pictures that way and alone. Then he laid them in Sen's arms with their blankets off and took one of her holding her babies. He couldn't wait to show the others his newest grandbabies.

His phone was passed around for about an hour. Cassie showed up just as he got it back and took it from him again. She, of course, cried not just for missing out on seeing them born but also that she was a grandma again. Everyone thought that they were too young to be grandparents, but he didn't care. They called him that, and he was thrilled beyond words that he had that title, too.

On the way home, Cassie was telling him about the special assignment she'd been asked to do. No names were given to him, but details. She had been assigned to fly a drone over some houses that the feds were fearful of making bombs and other explosives that were being built there.

"Even the main house on the farm was full of bomb making equipment that they were lucky it didn't explode with all the heat in the house. They were actually growing pot in the basement as well as storing large amounts of cocaine, too. It was a bomb just waiting for the opportunity to go off." He asked her what had happened to it. "When I left, they had hazmat there, taking things out one at a time. They're going to have to kill the animals that lived there as a decoy. One of the vets that had come along with us said that they'd been breathing that stuff in since birth and would need a fix like a newborn child would be if the mother had been doing drugs when she carried them. This world is messed up."

"I agree." Pulling into the garage when they got home, he was surprised to see a great many mail-order-like boxes on the front steps. "What have you ordered now? Not that I care, but I'm going to be the one that has to carry things in, so hopefully, it's not too heavy."

"It's the stuff that I ordered for the Fourth of July picnic that we're having. Mostly, it's paper plates and décor. I think that all of us getting together with the townspeople is going to be a yearly event. It's going to be that fantastic. I'm so glad that we thought of it before Caleb did. I love getting ahead of him." He did as well, and it had been like that since he'd come to this area to be with his family. "Oh, and Liz's things too. With her starting school this fall, she'll need to get uniforms and shoes. I can't believe our baby girl is ready to start first grade already."

Daniel refused to think about that. To him and his way of thinking, she was still just a baby telling him to read to her every night. His brothers had been making fun of him since it had been mentioned that she'd be dating in a few more years, and he'd slapped them in the back of the head. How dare they say something like that to him. She wasn't ever going to date, nor was she ever having sex. He was going to put his foot down with that notion.

~*~

Cassie sat by the headstone that proclaimed that her brother had lived for only a short period of time. He'd been thirty-one when he'd been killed. It still, after all these years, hurt her to remember that she had lost him. Like every time before, she brought him a small duck. She'd finally had to purchase a basket for them, there had been so many. It had been his favorite toy from baby until he was murdered. There had been hundreds of them in his house when she and Daniel had moved in.

Once she had all the weeds pulled from his gravesite, she leaned back in the chair that she'd brought with her so that she could rest a bit. Wiping away the tears that were coming more and more because she was pregnant again, she told Bradley that she loved him.

"Sen had her baby last week. Well, her babies. Two little girls and one son. We couldn't believe that she'd named her baby boy Daniel Benson Bradley Hutcheson. It's a mouthful, but I think he'll have no trouble growing into it. The girls are Emma Cassandra and Emily Grace. I love the names. You'd end up calling them EC and EG just to be confusing for us all." She laughed and noticed a couple sitting on the ground near a headstone similar to her brothers.

Cassie also knew that it was a baby girl who had been killed in a car accident along with her older brother. It must have been her birthday today. They had cake and candles there for her, too. She looked at her brother's grave again.

"The ex-president is in prison, much to his disappointment. He's told everyone that he sees that he was innocent of the things that they caught him at. But no one believed him, I guess. He can't have a trial, either. The government body doesn't want the public to know that they'd elected a murderer and he was in office for two terms." She saw the young woman coming toward her with a slice of cake in her hand. If she was here when they visited, they always shared what they had brought for their children.

"Meggie would have been three today, and Jess would have been nine." Cassie told her that her brother had been gone for just over six years. "Yes, well, it's hard on those of us that are left behind, don't you think? I miss them every day. Does the grief ever go away?"

"No, it does soften a bit more over time, but you still miss them, and it hurts." She nodded. This was the first time since Cassie had been seeing them here that they'd ever spoken of their losses. "There are days when I'll think of him and smile. Thinking about something he would have said to me before laughing like a braying jackass and it will bring a smile to my face. Then, other times, I can have the same thought about him, and I'll cry my heart out. But it's easier now, too. I have my own husband and children to help with it, the depression. Thankfully, I have an entire family of babies and adults around that I can hold, too." Nodding, the other woman looked away before turning toward her again.

"I've wanted to end my life every day. There are

days when I don't want to get out of my bed or take a shower. I find life, my life to be worthless. I couldn't keep my babies safe. What kind of woman can't keep her children safe? A bad mother is who." Cassie stood up and started to reach for the other woman. She then backed away from her when the gun suddenly appeared. "No, stay away from me. I know what I'm doing. Just eat the cake."

She looked down at the cake and then at what she had assumed was her husband slumped over the marker for their child. She didn't know what she was going to do but Cassie was not going to taste that cake. Not even at gunpoint.

"You killed your husband." She said that he was worthless anyway. "How did you come to that conclusion? He'd been with you every time you've come here. That has to be something."

"He comes here so that I don't get to do this. But I fooled him, didn't I? He thought that I'd just shot him in the head, but poisoning him was so much…He should have killed me when it happened." She asked her what she meant. "I killed my own family. Rusty blames me every day. Oh, he's too smart to come out and just say that I did it, but I know what he's thinking. That I'm a fucking murderer and should be put down like the dog that I am."

"And what does that have to do with killing me?" She told her that she was going to be taking her misery away for her, too. "I'm not miserable. I'm happy. Sad at times, but I'm not miserable at all. I come here to tell my brother about the things that had happened this week. Tell him what he's missing. I know that he can't hear me, but that doesn't stop me from telling him. It's a comfort to me. Please put the gun away, and no one else has to be hurt."

"What if I put my gun to my own head?" Putting her statement to good use, the gun was at her head before she could blink. "I want to die. No one will allow it. What am I going to do?"

She didn't want to die. She had when Bradley had been murdered, all she wanted to do was to end her life, so she sort of knew what the other woman was going through. Then she thought of the story that Tabby told her about meeting Joey for the first time. And smiled.

"Go ahead. Shoot yourself in the head. I won't stop you." The other woman looked confused. "Unless you'd rather I did it for you. I don't mind. I've killed before. As a Federal Officer, I've seen my fair share of deaths. Caused quite a few of them as well.

"You're a murderer?" She told her that all the deaths that had been done by her had been done to keep the world safer. Putting out her hand, Cassie asked for the gun so that she could shoot her. "You'd do that? Kill me?"

The gun was wavering enough that Cassie thought that she could snatch it from her without much effort. And no one else could be harmed. Telling her again that she'd do it had the woman backing up. Cassie took two steps toward her with each step that she took back.

"Unless you want me to use my gun." Just as she finished the sentence, Cassie had her gun pointed at the woman's head. "There is no way I'd be able to miss from this distance. It would be a clean shot if that's what you want. Using your gun would save me a great deal of paperwork. Seeing how you've already killed your husband — where are your other children? I just remembered your name being in the paper now. Victoria Coulter. It was mentioned in the paper that you had five little ones at home. Tell me what you did to them, and I'll make sure that if you didn't kill them too, they get put into a good home."

"He hid them away from me." Cassie felt a relief all over her body, hearing that the children were at least safe. "He's a dirty bastard for doing that, don't you think? It's why he had to die. They all have to — what are you doing? Put that phone away."

"I'm calling the police to have them go and look at your house to find the others. I'd surely hate for them to hear that their own mother had planned to kill them, too. Plus, their dad. You just hang on— Hello, yes, my name is Major Cassandra Watson, FBI. I have an address to give you for you to check on the welfare of the children of Hank and Victoria Coulter. I'm standing in front of her, and she has a gun pointed at me. I have one pointed at her as well." She was never so glad to hear Joey Phillips, her brother-in-law, put on the call for her. He asked her if she was all right. "I am, so far. Mr. Coulter is dead, I believe. Victoria poisoned him, she told me. And I have a slice of the same cake near me that she was insisting that I eat as well."

"Did she give you a reason why she killed her husband?" She told Joey what she'd said about him hiding the children from her so she'd not kill them. "And what did she say about killing you."

"She believes that I'd feel better about losing my brother if I was dead. She has also threatened to— what was that, Victoria?" She told her that she wanted her children to be brought to her. "I don't think that's even remotely going to happen. Since everyone in the station knows that you want to kill them, too. No, it's just you and me now. And Joey. If he comes here, he'd going to blow your head off for you because he loves me and is that good. You'll see. In just a few minutes, you'll be wishing that you'd stayed home today. Or not. I don't give a rat's ass how you feel about being shot in the head."

"Cassie, honey, you probably shouldn't piss off a woman holding a gun to your head. It might make her pull the trigger." She said that she was pissed off that she'd made it so that she'd not get to talk to her brother. "You're near your brother's headstone? Thank you for that. My ETA is four minutes. Do you think you can hold her off for that long?"

"I do, as a matter of fact. If you're going to use that high-powered rifle, then I'm going to need to know when so I can move out of the way." Cassie knew that there wasn't any way that she'd be in the way unless she stepped in front of Victoria. But if she could get the woman to give her the gun because she was afraid, then no one else had to die today. "Victoria, you're to stand very still, all right? They don't want you to be moving around when he kills you."

"What are you talking about? No one is going to kill me." Just then, a cruiser pulled into the parking lot just behind her car. "You really called the police on me? You bitch."

"Give me the gun, and I promise you that I'll tell the police that you cooperated with me. Otherwise, the man that you can see lining up his shot on the top of the cruiser is going to kill you. And I promise you, neither one of us will lose any sleep with you being dead." She looked at the cruiser and then down at the red dot on her chest. "He will kill you, Victoria. There is no doubt about that."

"Here. You win this time. But next time, I'm just going to shoot you and be done with it. Tell that man to stop putting dots on me." She took the gun away from her and put her hands atop her head like she asked her to do. "You're the meanest person that I've ever met. Even meaner than my mother-in-law, I'm thinking."

Flipping her over after putting her on the ground, Cassie had to lean over and puke her breakfast up before she could cuff the younger woman. By the time she was in cuffs, the other officers were there and she was helped up by Joey. All the time Victoria was being read her rights, she was telling them what a bitch she'd been to her.

"Are you all right?" She told Joey that she didn't know. "I've had Caleb bring in Daniel instead of him driving. He's a lousy drive to begin with. Being scared out of his mind would make him have an accident."

"Do you think that he'll be mad at me? While make-up sex is wonderful, I don't want him to ever... she was going to kill me with that cake, Joey. She didn't have any idea who I was, but she was going to kill me." He held her to his body while she cried. "I don't want to die, you know that, don't you? Also, I need to stop coming out here to talk to Bradley. He's more than likely pissed off at me too. Don't you think?"

"I hope so. No one is pissed off at you. Terrified out of their minds but not mad. Honey, that was the scariest call I've ever taken. You saved that woman's life." She nodded, still leaning on him. "When Daniel gets here, just let him talk or yell at you. Then allow him to check you over. Nothing has happened to you, but he won't believe that until he sees it for himself." She told him that she'd do that.

"All I could think about was how I'd not gotten to babysit my granddaughters yet. How I hadn't baked any cookies with Luke in a very long time." She looked up at him. "I'm going to retire from the FBI starting now. I don't want to be pulled from my family ever again. I know that I could be shot without being in the Feds, but I think that I'd stand a better chance of living if I was just a normal person like a parent who volunteers at school. Maybe I'll drive one of the school buses or something just to be near them.

Cassie was happy that he wasn't agreeing or disagreeing with what she was saying. What she wanted more than anything right now was Daniel. She looked down the hill from where they were standing and saw him.

Taking it easy so she'd not fall, she made her way to him as he came up the hill to her. She was sobbing, coming so close to losing all the time that they had left together. When he was close enough to touch her, he picked her up in his arms and swung her around several times before putting her on her feet to kiss her.

"I love you so much." He told her that he loved her too. "I'm done with the feds. I want to live my life with you. Seeing the world and playing with the babies for whatever time we have left. Can you handle that?"

"Yes. Forever, love. Forever."

~*~

Love conquers all. Caleb, Joey, Martin, Harlin, Sebastian and Daniel and their respective wives lived for decades after that day.

They were the richest people in the world with money, love and companionship.

AWARD WINNING, BESTSELLING AUTHOR

Kathi Barton, a winner of the Pinnacle Book Achievement Award and a best-selling author on Amazon and All Romance books, lives in Nashport, Ohio, with her husband, Paul. When not creating new worlds and romance, Kathi and her husband enjoy camping and going to auctions. She can also be seen at county fairs with her husband, an artist and potter.

Her muse, a cross between Jimmy Stewart and Hugh Jackman, brings her stories to life for her readers in a way that has them coming back time and again for more. Her favorite genre is paranormal romance, with a great deal of spice. You can visit Kathi online and drop her an email if you'd like. She loves hearing from her fans. aaronskiss@gmail.com.

Follow Kathi on her blog: http://kathisbartonauthor.blogspot.com/